D0953093

The
Hard Kind
of Promise

The
Hard Kind
of Promise

by Gina Willner-Pardo

CLARION BOOKS | HOUGHTON MIFFLIN HARCOURT

NEW YORK | BOSTON | 2010

CLARION BOOKS

215 Park Avenue South, New York, New York 10003

Copyright © 2010 by Gina Willner-Pardo

The text was set in Fournier MT Regular.

Clarion Books is an imprint of
Houghton Mifflin Harcourt Publishing Company.

www.hmhbooks.com

LIBRARY OF CONGRESS CATALOGING-IN-PUBLICATION DATA

Willner-Pardo, Gina.
The hard kind of promise / by Gina Willner-Pardo.   p. cm.
Summary: California seventh-graders Sarah and Marjorie made a promise in kindergarten to
always be friends, but Marjorie is weird and Sarah, wanting to be at least somewhat popular,
makes friends with a fellow choir member.
ISBN 978-0-547-24395-5

[1. Best friends—Fiction. 2. Friendship—Fiction. 3. Popularity—Fiction. 4. Individuality—
Fiction. 5. Middle schools—Fiction. 6. Schools—Fiction. 7. California—Fiction.] I. Title.
PZ7.W683675Har 2010

[Fic]—dc22   2009026204

Manufactured in the United States of America
DOC 10 9 8 7 6 5 4 3 2 1
4500221002

To Cara, Evan, and Robert,

with love

CHAPTER 1

SARAH FRANKLIN had been best friends with Marjorie Fingerhut for eight years. Sarah couldn't imagine life without Marjorie. Marjorie made her laugh. Marjorie didn't make a big deal out of how Sarah was picky about food and had to eat the carrots before the celery. Marjorie knew how Sarah felt without Sarah's having to tell her. Somehow, magically, Marjorie always just knew. It made the bad parts of seventh grade seem less bad when Sarah thought about how at least she and Marjorie had each other.

Which made the problem Sarah was having especially hard.

They had met in preschool, when Sarah kept noticing Marjorie, who repeatedly told everyone at show-and-tell that she was a leprechaun. But it was in kindergarten, when they were five, that Sarah had really come to understand how it was with her and Marjorie. They were coloring at the Fingerhuts' kitchen table. The air around them smelled of the peanut butter from their sandwiches.

"It's fun being best friends," Marjorie had said. She was concentrating on her drawing and not looking at Sarah when she said it.

"It's really fun," Sarah had said. It felt as though her heart had exploded and little pieces of confetti-happiness were raining down over her insides.

"We should be best friends forever," Marjorie said.

"We should promise," Sarah said. Solemnly she added, "I promise to be best friends with you forever."

"I promise to be best friends with *you* forever," Marjorie said, giggling.

Sarah giggled, too, because it was fun, and also because Marjorie's always needing to repeat everything in a loud voice was one of the things that made her Marjorie, one of the things that Sarah loved.

Now, remembering that afternoon filled Sarah with a longing that was both piercing and inexplicable, and a little bit like dread.

In most ways, Sarah was happy to be in seventh grade. There were no little kids running around at recess, no lining up to come in from lunch, no Mr. Wheatley for PE. Everyone got five different teachers, so even if you got Mrs. Fogelson for math, it didn't matter, because you only had to sit there for fifty minutes. Then you got to go to another classroom with another teacher, who maybe wasn't perfect but was definitely better than Mrs. Fogelson, who had nose hairs.

After a year of stressful self-consciousness in sixth grade, Sarah had grown to like the way she looked. Her blond hair had darkened in the past year or two: now it was honey-colored, almost but not quite brown. It came to just above her shoulders; she parted it in the middle and blow-dried it straight every other morning. She liked her hair in the same way that she liked her eyes (hazel, with dark lashes) and her nose (not too big, lightly freckled) and her feet (small, with a prominent second toe, which she had once read was a sign of intelligence). She wasn't too crazy about her invisible cheekbones, the mole on her shoulder, or the fact that she hadn't gotten any taller since fifth grade. But overall, she was pretty satisfied.

Another good thing about seventh grade was chorus. In fifth grade, kids could only take band. Ms. Washington let them pick any instrument they wanted and made them switch only if there were too many flutes or not enough French horns. They gave a concert in the spring. From the clarinet section, Sarah thought they sounded horrible, but Dad and his new wife, Diane, said they were good. Mom didn't come. She still didn't like going places where she might run into Diane.

Sarah switched from band to chorus in sixth grade. It was so much better. Even if they sometimes sang out of tune, at least it sounded like singing. Band sounded like sick animals. Sarah loved standing in a semicircle around Mr. Roche, watching his hands to help her keep the time, trying to remember about posture and not tapping her foot and not singing through her nose. There was a lot to remember, but Sarah didn't mind. She loved "Shenandoah" and "Amazing Grace" and "She Walks in Beauty." "All Star" by Smash Mouth gave her goose bumps, even though Mr. Roche put it in the repertoire just to keep the boys interested.

Marjorie didn't switch to chorus. She kept playing bassoon in the seventh grade band, along with Dennis Veitch, who had been taking private lessons since second grade and was first chair. Marjorie didn't mind. She played louder than Dennis until the band director had to make everyone else stop and tell Marjorie to "pipe down." Everyone would laugh, but it never bothered Marjorie.

Nothing ever bothered Marjorie.

Which was part of the problem.

In seventh grade chorus, Sarah mostly hung out with Lizzie Lowitz, who had gone to a different elementary school. Sarah really liked Lizzie. She had long, black, frizzy hair and was totally boy crazy. When Mr. Roche gave the altos a break, Sarah and Lizzie would sit in the corner and talk about the boys in the class. "He is so cute," Lizzie would say about everyone, except Jason Webb, who already had a beard. "That hair on his face is gross. It has food in it," she would whisper. "We hate him." And even though Sarah didn't hate Jason—didn't even know him—she would laugh, because it was fun to gossip, to talk about things that she never talked about with Marjorie, who was still wearing shirts with cartoon characters on them and didn't seem to know that boys were even alive.

Even though she had a lot of fun with Lizzie, when the lunch bell rang, Sarah headed over to the far side of the school, where Marjorie had staked out a bench under a lone palm tree. They liked sitting there: they could see what everyone was doing, but they were far enough away that no one bothered them. They talked about who said dumb things in class and wondered what their teachers did in their own houses after school. They laughed at Mrs. Gretch, who was both the assistant principal and the special skills teacher, because during all the breaks she went out to her car and smoked with the windows up. When she got out of the car, smoke poured out behind her, as if she'd started a campfire in there.

They talked about their families. They told old jokes. They remembered things. There was a lot to remember, after eight years. Sarah always remembered that Marjorie was the girl in preschool with magic shoes that made her fast, the girl who saw fairies and sprinkled crushed-up barbecue potato chips onto her peanut butter sandwich. And how in third grade Marjorie was the girl who wore Tweety Bird T-shirts and purple stretch pants three days in a row, even after Alison Mulvaney said cartoon characters were babyish, even Bart Simpson.

Some things Sarah remembered and didn't talk about. How Marjorie never seemed to notice when other kids made fun of her lazy eye. How it was Marjorie who invited Sarah over after school every day for a month when Sarah's dad moved out. And how, around Christmas last year, when Grandpa had to have his right leg amputated, Marjorie knew without being told that Sarah was really afraid of seeing his stump. Sarah never had to say. Marjorie just knew.

"Mrs. Gretch is not pwetty," Marjorie still said sometimes, using her Tweety Bird voice, and Sarah giggled, because it was still funny when she did it. But secretly she was glad they were sitting on the faraway bench, that no one else was around to hear.

Marjorie's favorite class was video production. Each kid got to learn how to make movies, and Marjorie loved movies. She knew most of the lines from *Star Wars* by heart. She had seen *The Matrix Reloaded* fifteen times and *Alien vs. Predator* eighteen times. Also, she watched old movies on TV when her parents thought she was asleep. Science fiction movies were her favorite, but she would watch anything in black-and-white: westerns and musicals and just plain old stories with men wearing hats and talking in a way that real people never talked. Sometimes when Sarah spent the night, they would sneak down to the family room and turn on the TV just to see what was on. Marjorie knew the names of all the old movie stars and which ones had won Oscars and how many times they'd been married.

"How do you know all this stuff?" Sarah asked her once as they lay on the floor on their stomachs, on big pillows that they'd pulled off the couch. The room was dark except for the flickery blue light of the TV. The clock on the DVD player said it was 3:31 in the morning.

"I read books," Marjorie said. "And my grandma knows all about old movies. She watched them when they weren't old."

Grandma Fingerhut lived in Ohio, but she came out to the Bay Area for Christmas and birthdays. Sarah was a little afraid of her because she was always asking questions to find out if Sarah had gotten her period yet. But she was Marjorie's favorite relative except for her parents. They talked like friends, not like a kid and an old person.

"Grandma says she would have been a director if they'd let women do that in the old days," Marjorie said. "She says I'm lucky *I* don't have to work in a school cafeteria."

"Do you want to be a director?" Sarah asked.

Marjorie nodded. "Or maybe a sound editor."

"What's a sound editor?"

"The person who figures out what music goes with what scene. It makes a huge difference in the movie. Think about what *Star Wars* would be like without the music."

Sarah tried to imagine.

"I never thought of that," she said. "I never thought of the music as something separate."

"That's because the sound editor did a good job."

On the TV, a man and woman in fancy clothes danced to an old-fashioned love song in a garden. They were singing the words to the song and they weren't even out of breath. Marjorie was mouthing the words along with them.

"You'd be a good sound editor," Sarah said. She was impressed that Marjorie had thought of such an unusual job. Most kids wanted to be doctors or lawyers or soccer players.

"What do you want to be?" Marjorie asked.

"I don't know yet."

"If you could be anything. If you could wave a magic wand and just *be* something."

"Maybe a singer. If I get better."

It wasn't true, but Sarah was too embarrassed to say what she really wanted to be.

Marjorie knew she was lying.

"What else?" she asked.

After a minute Sarah said, "It's not very glamorous."

Marjorie shrugged, not taking her eyes off the dancing couple.

"It probably doesn't pay very much," Sarah said.

"So?"

"My mom says I should try to make a lot of money. She says you shouldn't let someone else support you. She says you never know."

"Yeah, but Sarah, you have to be *happy*."

"Well, maybe I can be happy making a lot of money."

"Yeah." Marjorie was quiet for a few minutes. Then she asked, "What's the other job, anyway?"

Sarah waited until the music was over and the dancing lady's floaty dress had stopped swirling.

"You know when my grandpa had his leg amputated and he had to go to physical therapy? Well, there were all these people who helped him do exercises so he could walk on his fake leg. And so his other muscles were strong." She paused. "I might like to help people like that."

Suddenly she felt shy.

"Is it like PE?" Marjorie asked. "Because you hate PE."

"No. I don't have to do the exercises. I just have to help other people do them." On TV, the dancing couple were having a fight, but you could tell they would make up, that they really loved each other. "I think I might like helping people," Sarah said.

Without taking her eyes off the screen, Marjorie said, "I think you'd be really good at that."

They watched the movie in silence. Sarah felt happy, the way you did when you told somebody something important and she didn't laugh.

When the couple finally kissed, Marjorie said, "See,

if I'd directed this movie, there'd have been a big blue space alien in it. With eyestalks."

"It would have been better that way," Sarah said, just to be nice.

Marjorie nodded. "That's what I think, too," she said.

A week later, at lunch, Alison and Zannie Pierce and Yvonne Brondello approached Sarah and Marjorie's palm tree. As they came closer and closer, Sarah felt her heart begin to pound. Alison practically ran the school. There was no reason for her to want to talk to them.

"You guys have to move," Alison said, looking down at them as if they were something that had gotten stuck on her shoe. "This bench is too big for just two people."

"You can sit here," Marjorie said, picking up her lunch bag and scrunching closer to the edge of the bench. "There's room."

"What smells?" Yvonne said, crinkling up her nose. "It smells gross over here."

"Her lunch," Zannie said, pointing. "She still eats gross things."

Yvonne, whose mother ran Mama Brondello's Cooking with Love Catering Service, looked disgusted. "You shouldn't eat egg salad. It goes bad in the heat," she said. "Doesn't your mom know about not making sandwiches with mayonnaise?"

"My dad makes my lunch," Marjorie said.

Alison, Zannie, and Yvonne all giggled in a nasty way. Zannie whispered something to Yvonne, who laughed out loud.

Alison turned back to Marjorie. "You need to move," she said.

"We were here first," Sarah said. She could hear the shaking in her voice.

"In about ten seconds, all the leadership people are going to get here. And there isn't enough room for all of us." Alison put her hands on her hips, which—Sarah couldn't help but notice—had begun to look like an adult's. "Do you really want to explain to them how you were here first?"

The leadership people were all the kids who were elected to school offices. There was a president, a few vice presidents, a secretary, and a treasurer. Each class also had a representative. They had a lot of meetings and decided things like whether you should have to get dressed up for the eighth grade dances or could just go in jeans. Alison was the seventh grade rep.

"Why do you have to sit in our place?" Sarah asked. She glanced over at Marjorie, wishing she would say something, but Marjorie just smiled fiercely, the way she did when someone was being mean.

Alison sighed. "I don't want to have to explain everything," she said. "Just move."

"And fast," Yvonne said. "That egg salad smell is making me sick."

Sarah and Marjorie gathered up their lunches and their backpacks. Sarah really wished Marjorie's didn't have decals that read SCIENCE FICTION RULES and BEAM ME UP, SCOTTY plastered all over it. She could feel the other girls' nasty stares even without looking at their faces.

Standing up, she faced Alison. "This is still our place. We're eating here tomorrow, no matter what you say."

Alison opened her mouth as if to speak. Sarah braced herself but was surprised when Alison closed her mouth and gave a small, smug smile, then shrugged her shoulders, as though Sarah could say whatever she wanted, but it was obvious who had the power, who had ended up with the bench.

"Marjorie," Sarah said as they ventured out onto the hot, crowded playground, "you shouldn't be so nice about letting them sit with us when they were so mean."

"Why?"

Sarah sighed. The way Marjorie didn't get things could be frustrating.

"Because sometimes, the nicer you are, the meaner they are. Don't you get that?" She scanned the schoolyard, trying to find an empty bench. "No wonder they wanted our place. Everything else is taken."

"We can sit on the edge of the soccer field," Marjorie said.

The only kids who hung out that far from the classrooms were the kids with no friends, either because they'd just moved to the school or didn't speak English or did really weird things like pick their noses or walk down the halls talking to themselves.

"I don't think we should sit out there," Sarah said. "Why?"

It was hard to explain this kind of thing to Marjorie. The unwritten rules that everyone else understood without batting an eye just didn't make sense to her. She was always asking "Why?" or "So what?" Sometimes it felt to Sarah as though Marjorie really *was* a space alien who'd gotten lost in the universe and was beamed down to the wrong planet.

Marjorie pushed at her glasses, which were sliding down her nose. "Come on," she said. "It's hot, and I'm still hungry!"

Sarah trudged along behind her, sure that every

kid on the playground was watching them make their way across the soccer field. She decided that she wasn't ever doing this again, that even if Alison pointed a gun at her, she wasn't getting up from their bench.

The sun was hot, but she was even hotter, and it wasn't the weather. It came from misery, from embarrassment, from having been sent away, from having nowhere else to go. Ahead of her, Marjorie walked on, completely oblivious.

It occurred to Sarah that if it weren't for her, Marjorie might be the kind of kid who ate all her lunches out on the edge of the soccer field.

That was the first time Sarah had ever really thought about it. Except for her, Marjorie had no friends.

She wasn't exactly sure why. Marjorie was the nicest person Sarah had ever known. She was Sarah's favorite person. She was her best friend.

She wasn't weirder than other kids. Carl Estes screwed the head off his sister's Barbie doll and ate it once, and he had friends. They thought it was cool when he had to go to the emergency room and have an operation to get the Barbie head out.

But Carl did sports: soccer and basketball and then baseball in the spring. Sports made kids like you. Even if you were weird or mean, other kids liked you if you were good at sports.

Marjorie was terrible at sports. She was even bad at skipping. She was the only kid who couldn't do one pushup for the President's Physical Fitness Test in fifth grade. Mr. Wheatley kept giving her more chances, which just made it worse, because all the kids stood around watching and laughing, and no matter how many chances she had, Marjorie couldn't do one pushup. Not one. After a while it felt as though Mr. Wheatley wasn't really giving her more chances. It felt as though he was punishing her.

Girls cared if you were good at sports, and also about how pretty you were and what kinds of clothes you wore. Marjorie was pretty, Sarah thought loyally. She had soft, wavy brown hair and big blue eyes and beautiful skin and a pretty smile. And her hair smelled like pineapples. But it was longer than Alison's shoulder-length hair and too wavy to stay neat. Marjorie always looked like she'd just gotten out of a convertible, the way her hair was all blown around.

Her lazy eye wasn't so lazy anymore, but her glasses made it hard to tell. And her perfect skin was pale and milky—not tan like Alison's, from being on swim team.

It wasn't enough to be pretty. You had to be pretty

in the right way. And your clothes had to be right, too. If your skirts were too short, you might look trampy. If they were too long, you might be a hippie, which, according to the popular girls, was very bad, even though no one was actually sure what a hippie was. Your jeans had to be the right kind of jeans. If you wanted to be popular, you had to have the right kind of sunglasses. If you didn't care about being popular, the worst thing you could do was wear sunglasses, even cool ones, because then it would look as though secretly you really *did* want to be popular, which was worse than not wanting to be popular at all.

There were a lot of rules, and no one explained them to you. You were just supposed to know.

The weirdest thing of all was how everyone had just decided that Alison was the most popular girl in Sarah's class. She wasn't prettier than other girls, and she certainly wasn't nicer. Most people didn't even like her. But somehow, everyone cared what she thought.

Well, almost everyone.

The day after they had to eat at the edge of the soccer field, Sarah was in the girls' bathroom between second and third periods.

The room was empty when she entered the stall, but while she was in there, Alison and Yvonne came in to brush their hair. Alison brushed her hair before every period. While she did it, she talked about everything that was wrong with how she looked, even though you could tell that she didn't really think *anything* was wrong with how she looked. Sarah could see them through the slit in the stall door.

"My hair is so unbelievably gross," Alison said, running a brush through it, tipping her head so that her ear was almost parallel to the floor. "It's so split-end-y."

"It is not," Yvonne said. "It's beautiful. Look how smooth it is."

Sarah felt sorry for Yvonne, who had thin rust-colored hair that hung like string around her round cheeks.

"It's just, I don't know. It's not shiny enough. It's not like in those ads where the model runs her hands through her hair and it *glitters,*" Alison said.

"Like diamonds," Yvonne said dreamily. Then, because Alison was glaring at her, she said, "Your hair totally does that."

Sarah could see from inside the stall that Alison had stopped brushing her hair and was looking at herself in the mirror.

"Well, maybe a little," she said.

Yvonne, whose hair-brushing didn't take nearly as long as Alison's, returned her brush to her backpack and said, "My mom says you can put mayonnaise in your hair to make it shiny."

Alison looked horrified. "You mean, like what you *eat?*"

Yvonne nodded. "It's like a conditioner, only better. You let it sit for a while and then rinse it off. And your hair just glows."

"Really?" Alison's eyes got small and suspicious. "Have you tried it?"

"Once. I smelled like salad dressing. And nothing works on my hair," Yvonne said sadly. "But my mom swears it works. She says movie stars do it all the time. You should try it. Your hair's so much prettier than mine. I'm sure it'll work on you."

Alison shrugged, as though she had better things to do than sit around soaking in mayonnaise anyway, so why were they even talking about it? Then she laughed.

"Maybe that's what Marjorie does with all the mayonnaise at her house. That her dad's not using for sandwiches."

Sarah froze, suddenly afraid that they could see her through the slit in the door.

Yvonne snickered. "Maybe that's why it always smells around her, even when she's not eating. Maybe it's all that bad mayonnaise."

Alison shook her head, checking, Sarah could tell, to see if her hair was glittering from all the brushing.

"She is so weird."

"It's like she *likes* being weird. Like she wants to be weird on purpose."

That's not true! Sarah shouted in her head. Marjorie wasn't trying to be weird. She couldn't help it.

Alison tipped her head. "I think there's really something wrong with her. Like, *mentally* wrong."

Yvonne's eyes got big. "Really? You think she's retarded?"

Sarah hated that word. Her mom taught handicapped kids at a special school. She said "retarded" was a mean word. And that everyone was smart in his own way.

"Maybe." Alison leaned in close to the mirror, checking for pimples. "Her head's too big, don't you think?"

"I guess so." Yvonne sounded unsure. "But I have her in math. She usually knows the right answer."

Unlike you, Sarah thought, who hasn't known the right answer since first grade.

"Well, something's wrong with her. I don't know exactly what." Alison straightened up and gave herself a look in the mirror to make sure that she looked just the way she wanted to. "But something."

They headed for the door.

"I don't get why Sarah likes her," Yvonne said.

"Losers always like each other," Alison said.

CHAPTER 2

L O S E R . That's what Alison called her. A loser.

Losers were the worst. In middle school, losers were at the bottom, even below the weird kids, who usually had something going for them, like accidentally being funny in class or being geniuses. Losers had nothing.

Sarah was in shock. She couldn't believe anyone thought she was a loser. She knew she wasn't popular. But she always thought she was somewhere in the middle. A girl that most people sort of liked because there was no reason not to like her. She looked average, with almost brown hair and hazel eyes with yellow flecks in them that sometimes made them look green. There was that mole on her shoulder, but no one could even see it, except in the summer. And besides, she tried to be nice. She didn't have bad breath. She didn't smell.

Uh-oh, she thought, hurrying a little through the crowds in the hall, knowing the bell was about to ring. What if the smell of Marjorie's weird lunches is sticking to me? Maybe people think that *I* smell like tuna or egg salad.

Maybe Marjorie is rubbing off on me.

So what? she thought, trying to be like Marjorie, trying not to care. So what if Alison thinks I'm a loser? I don't even have any classes with her. I don't even see her in the halls most days.

So what? she thought, but it was hopeless.

She was still upset in chorus.

"What's the matter?" Lizzie whispered. Mr. Roche was working with the boys.

Something wouldn't let Sarah tell Lizzie. She was too ashamed, and too afraid of what Lizzie might say.

"Do you like these jeans?" she asked instead.

Lizzie gave Sarah's legs a serious look.

"Yeah. I especially like the way the pockets look."

"Really?" Sarah looked down. She had never thought about pockets.

"My jeans are heinous," Lizzie said. "My mom makes me buy them on sale."

Sarah's mom did, too, but she didn't feel like saying so just then. "Do you want to walk down to the

Juice Warehouse after school?" she asked. It was the first time she had ever suggested they do anything together. She held her breath. It was always risky to change the way things were.

Lizzie smiled. "Sure," she said. "Only I can't drink wheatgrass. Wheatgrass is heinous."

"Heinous" was Lizzie's new word. Sarah decided in that instant that she loved it, even though she wasn't exactly sure what it meant.

"I like the peach-strawberry smoothie," she said. "They'll put in extra peaches if you ask."

Mr. Roche held up his arms and snapped his fingers.

"Altos, I need you!" he said.

"Meet you at the flagpole," Lizzie whispered.

At lunch, Marjorie was bubbling with excitement.

"We get to make a three-minute film in video production!" she said before Sarah even had a chance to sit down. "It can be about anything we want! I'm going to get Louellen to make me a blue space-alien costume! She has to hurry, because the film is due the day before Thanksgiving break."

Marjorie's sister Louellen was in college. She was really good at sewing.

"Three minutes doesn't sound very long," Sarah said grumpily.

"It is long when you think about everything a director has to do," Marjorie said importantly. "Write the script. Decide what the scene will look like. Pick the cast. Pick the music—"

"Okay, okay, I get it." Immediately Sarah felt bad. She was just suddenly sick of being best friends with someone other people didn't like. She couldn't help it.

To try to make it up to Marjorie, she asked, "What's your movie going to be about?"

Marjorie began to peel a bruised-looking banana.

"This big blue space alien lands on Earth. He's been sent by his planet to study other forms of intelligent life in the universe, and he lands right here, on the Keith Middle School playground."

"He's going to have to look pretty hard to find intelligent life."

Not laughing, Marjorie went on.

"The kids are really nice to him. They show him all the classrooms and talk about what their lives are like. No one can take him home, because they're afraid of what their parents would think, so they build him a bed in Mr. Mayberry's room, under the Bunsen burners."

"But wouldn't the teachers be as suspicious as the parents?"

"I'm not going to have any teachers in it. That would be too hard to arrange."

"But I'm just saying. The teachers would know if a blue space alien had landed at the school. Wouldn't they call the police?"

Marjorie put down her banana and took a bite of her pastrami-sprinkled-with-barbecue-potato-chips sandwich.

"No, because the kids will find him first. They'll hide him."

"But—"

"Sarah, you'll see. It'll work out. I have it all planned."

They ate in silence. Sarah was keeping an eye out for Alison and the leadership kids, but they were nowhere in sight. She tried to feel triumphant about getting their place under the palm tree back, but it was hard: she kept remembering how Alison had called her a loser. She watched groups of other kids—boys shooting baskets, threesomes of girls giggling and shrieking—and wondered if they knew her name, if they'd heard of her, what opinions of her they might hold. The sound of Marjorie chomping on her sandwich was really getting on her nerves.

"So," Marjorie said, accidentally spitting a crumb of barbecue potato chip as she spoke, "you want to be the space alien?"

"You mean, in your movie?"

"Louellen will make the costume to fit you. You'll be the star."

Sarah was going to say no. Being an alien in one of Marjorie's movies was about the last thing she felt like doing. But she couldn't deny that she liked the idea of being a star.

"Who else is going to be in it?" she asked.

"Me. And maybe Joey Hooper. Joey's going to help me direct."

"How can you have two directors for one movie?"

"Lots of people do it. Michael and Peter Spierig both directed *The Undead*."

"Who's Joey Hooper?"

"A new kid. He's in video production. He asked me to be in his movie, so I might ask him to be in mine."

Sarah liked it that Marjorie had someone else to be in the movie besides just the two of them.

"Is he nice?" she asked.

Marjorie shrugged. "He's okay."

Sarah took a breath.

"Is he cute?"

Marjorie fumbled in her lunch bag. "Hey, do you have grapes?" she asked. "Grapes are better with pastrami than a banana."

Sarah sighed. Clearly, Marjorie was not ready to talk about boys.

"No. Just an apple," she said. After a moment she said, "I'll be the alien."

It actually almost sounded like fun.

"As long as we do it after school and on weekends," she added. "I don't want to be running around in a blue alien costume at lunch."

"Why not?"

"*Because*. Because it's weird, okay? Because I don't want to do anything that weird in front of other people."

Marjorie poked her glasses back up on her nose and smiled.

"Okay," she said.

Sarah wished she didn't have to explain everything. She wished Marjorie just got it, the way everyone else did. She wished she didn't have to hurt Marjorie's feelings to protect herself.

"You want to meet after school and scout locations?" Marjorie asked.

Sarah remembered Lizzie.

"I can't today," she said. "I have a dentist appointment."

"Another one? Already?"

"I have a lot of cavities," Sarah said. She could feel herself blushing with the lie she was telling. "Five, actually."

"Wow. Five." Marjorie crumpled up her lunch bag. "I've only had two in my whole life."

"You're lucky."

The bell rang. They rose from the bench.

"Do you really think all the kids would be nice to the space alien?" Sarah asked as they threw their bags into the trash can.

"Sure," Marjorie said, pushing at her glasses again. "Why wouldn't they be?"

That night, Grandpa came for dinner at Mom's. He still used a cane sometimes, but he'd gotten pretty used to his prosthetic leg in the past year and was proud of how well he walked and also of having almost all his hair. He was tall and muscular and made sure to stand straight, even when he was tired.

"Hey, Sarah," he said, "can I have a hug?"

He always asked, another thing Sarah loved.

Henry the poodle, his fur still curly and black but beginning to turn a distinguished shade of gray, pranced into the hallway, his tail wagging. Mom had gotten him when she and Dad divorced, hoping that he would be a good guard dog. He was terrible. The only thing he barked at was the sound of motorcycles on the street below.

"Hey, buddy. How's my buddy?" Grandpa asked, rubbing Henry's puffballed head.

Henry panted with the pleasure of being rubbed. Then he ducked down low, rear end high in the air, ready to play.

"Not now, Henry," Sarah said. But Henry ignored her. He wagged his tail and looked hopefully at Grandpa.

"That damn dog," Grandpa said. "Henry. Cut it out."

Sarah and Grandpa watched as Henry held his ground, rump still raised, hoping that someone would give in and roll a ball for him to fetch.

"Poodles are really smart," Sarah said. "He knows exactly what we're saying."

"I'm going to do a little research on the computer," Grandpa said. "See if we can't find a way to make Henry mind."

Sarah smiled as they headed toward the kitchen. Grandpa loved any excuse to look things up online.

Mom had already poured his cranberry juice, which was sitting on the kitchen counter. Grandpa was an alcoholic. He hadn't had a drink in seventeen years, but he said that didn't matter, that he would be an alcoholic until the day he died. Sarah was proud of him for not drinking anymore and also for being honest about who he was. She liked hearing his stories from the old days, when he used to hang out in bars, even though Mom didn't like for him to say too much and was always trying to change the subject.

"You look tired, Dad," Mom said. She was pulling strands of silk from corncobs and wearing her KISS THE COOK apron, which was from when she was still married to Sarah's dad and which Sarah wished she wouldn't wear anymore.

"Nope. Just need to sit down," Grandpa said, reaching for his juice and pulling a chair out from the table. Henry, who had followed them into the kitchen, waited until Grandpa was settled and then lowered himself to the floor at his feet. He liked sitting wherever Grandpa was because sometimes Grandpa was a sloppy eater and dropped food on the floor.

"How's school?" Grandpa asked Sarah.

"Okay."

"How's singing?"

"Pretty good. It's my favorite class." He already knew, but Sarah said it anyway. "We're working on a round. That's where you sing lines and then another few kids sing the same lines, only later. It's hard to keep track of where you are."

"We did that," Grandpa said. "'Row, Row, Row Your Boat.'"

"We did that, too. In kindergarten. This is harder than that," Sarah said.

"You just have to focus on your own voice. On where you are in the music. Don't think about what the others are singing." Grandpa liked to give advice, which got on Sarah's nerves sometimes, but she knew he meant well.

"It's hard to hear myself over everyone else," she said.

"I know," Grandpa said. "It gets easier."

He said it as though he was sure, even though she knew he'd never sung in public in his life.

"Sarah's got a new friend from chorus," Mom said. She was standing over the open oven door, checking on the spareribs. "What's her name, honey?"

Sarah hated how her mother still cared so much about who her friends were. Mom liked Marjorie, but she always said it was good to have more than one friend. You never know, she said, which is what she said about almost everything. Mom lived as though she thought some catastrophe was going to happen in the next hour and she wanted to be prepared.

"Lizzie." To Grandpa, Sarah said, "She's not a friend, exactly. Just someone I hang out with."

"Of course she's a friend!" Mom said.

"Why isn't she a friend?" Grandpa asked.

"Because—because . . ." It was so hard to explain. "Because Marjorie's my friend."

"Can't you have more than one friend?" Grandpa asked.

"Well, yeah, if you're all friends together."

"Why can't Marjorie and this Lizzie be friends?" Grandpa asked.

She waited for him to finish his juice before she answered.

"I don't know if they'd like each other," she said. "Marjorie can be kind of annoying."

"But you like her," Grandpa said.

Mom brought over the salad bowl and set three plates on the table.

"Maybe it's time you and Marjorie took a little time apart," she said.

"No!" Sarah said. She noticed with irritation that there were artichokes in the salad. Mom knew she hated artichokes. "She's my best friend! You don't take time apart when you're best friends."

Grandpa used the salad tongs to put salad on Sarah's plate.

"Remember Patty Bowlingball?" he asked, winking at Mom.

Patty Bolenbaugh was Mom's best friend when she was a kid. Grandpa had always called her Patty Bowlingball as a joke. Mom still rolled her eyes when he said it.

"What about her?" Mom asked.

"Your mother and I thought you two spent too much time together. Especially when Patty decided it was time the two of you got your ears pierced. Remember?" Grandpa looked at Sarah. "Your grandmother about had a fit. She wanted to send your mother to a private school. Split them up for good."

"Why didn't she?" Sarah had heard it before, but Grandpa loved to talk about Mom when she was little.

"When she heard about being sent to a private school, your mother moped around for a week. Wouldn't talk. Wouldn't eat. 'Patty's my best friend,' she kept saying." Grandpa speared a cucumber with his fork. "Finally your grandmother just gave up."

Mom swallowed a small bite of salad. "Well, for heaven's sake, Dad, I'm not saying Sarah should go to another *school*." She poked around on her plate, looking for a crouton. "I'm just saying you can't have too many friends."

"But it's not like that in middle school," Sarah said. "You have one best friend and then maybe a couple of other people you hang out with. Not big groups, though."

"I had a big group," Grandpa said.

"Boys are different."

Grandpa laughed. "Maybe so," he said.

Mom stood up to check on the spareribs again. "Well, I had lots of friends," she said, opening the oven door. "Why don't you try introducing Marjorie and Lizzie? Maybe they'll like each other."

"I don't know," Sarah said. "I don't know Lizzie well enough yet."

Lizzie and Sarah had had a pretty good time at the Juice Warehouse, but there were a lot of silences. It was hard to think of what to say to a new person. With Marjorie, there was always something to talk about: movies, old jokes, memories.

"When I first got my prosthesis, I tried to hide it," Grandpa said. "I didn't tell people about it. When I'd walk into a store and the clerk would ask me about my limp, I'd just say I'd twisted my knee. Now I tell everyone. In the summer I wear shorts. I don't care what people say."

Sarah sighed. "It's different in middle school," she said. "You have to care what people say, or no one will like you."

"Oh, Sarah," Mom said from over by the oven, where she was putting spareribs on their plates. She sounded frustrated. It bugged Sarah that her mom acted as though it wasn't that way when she was in middle school, which it definitely was, even if everyone was still dancing to disco and no one had computers.

"What would Lizzie say about Marjorie?" Grandpa asked.

"That she's weird."

"Is she?" he asked.

Sarah looked away. "A little."

Grandpa laughed as Mom set his plate in front of him. "Good for her," he said. "And good for you for liking her anyway."

Mom gave Sarah her plate. "There are lots of non-weird people to like, you know," she said. "There's nothing wrong with being *normal*."

"Mom," Sarah said. She was so irritating.

Grandpa picked up a rib and took a bite. A little barbecue sauce got into his mustache.

"As I recall, Patty Bowlingball liked to tell people she could bend spoons just by thinking about them," he said. "Now *that's* weird."

Sarah gave him a grateful look. She didn't tell him that she wouldn't mind if Marjorie could find a way to be just a little less weird.

CHAPTER 3

IN CHORUS THE NEXT DAY, Mr. Roche asked everyone to sit down. Sarah knew this meant they weren't going to sing. You had to stand for singing.

"We have a very exciting opportunity," Mr. Roche said. He was younger than Sarah's parents, and pudgy, and he wore big tinted glasses indoors, which made him look like pictures of men from the 1970s. Also, he had a nose ring.

Lizzie leaned close and whispered, "Uh-oh. Something's going on. I'll bet it means extra work."

Mr. Roche crossed his arms and stared at Lizzie. Usually he tried to act as though he were one of the kids, but when someone whispered in class, he got just as mad as any other teacher.

When Lizzie was quiet, he went on.

"We have been asked to participate in a choral competition in Los Angeles," he said.

Everyone started talking at once. Going to Los Angeles meant flying and staying overnight.

"People, please!" Mr. Roche begged. "Raise your hands if you have questions."

Jason Webb raised his hand and then, without waiting to be called on, asked, "Can we go to Disneyland?"

Lizzie looked at Sarah and shook her head. "He is beyond heinous," she said. Then she added, "Hey, if we get to stay in a motel, do you want to be in my room?"

"Definitely," Sarah said, feeling happy.

Mr. Roche was rapping on his music stand with his baton.

"If you are not quiet in the next three seconds, we will not be going to Los Angeles," he said sternly.

Immediately everyone shut up.

"Traveling as a chorus means that we will have to *listen* to each other. That we will have to *follow directions*. That we will have to be *respectful* of *adults*." Mr. Roche pushed his shaggy bangs off his forehead. "Do you think you can handle that?"

Everyone said yes together. Jason Webb raised his hand.

"Yes?" Mr. Roche said.

"What about Disneyland?" Jason asked.

"There isn't going to be time for Disneyland. And you all need to understand that this competition is going to mean a lot of extra rehearsal time."

Without turning her head, Lizzie whispered, "Told you so."

"We're going to have to meet after school and on some Saturdays," Mr. Roche said. "If you have other commitments, you're not going to be able to make rehearsals. And if you can't make rehearsals, you can't go to Los Angeles."

Molly Worth raised her hand. "What about soccer?" she asked. "I have soccer games every Saturday."

"Well, you're going to have to think about that, Molly," Mr. Roche said. "Chorus isn't just a class. Chorus is a commitment, and it's just as important as swim team and horseback riding and soccer and chess club."

"There's no horseback riding here," Jason said.

Lizzie sighed loudly. "Not at school, but some people ride horses," she said. *"God!"*

"Shut up!" Jason said.

Lizzie turned around. "You shut up," she said. "And shave, why don't you?"

"That's enough!" Mr. Roche slammed his baton down again. "This is exactly what I'm talking about!

This is the kind of thing we have to deal with if you guys want to win this competition. Now, I want you to think about it. There are going to be choruses from all over the state at this competition. They are going to be very serious about doing well. And I'm asking you all: Do you want to do this? Do you want to invest time and energy into becoming the best chorus you can possibly be?"

Lizzie looked irritated at having to agree with Jason Webb about anything, but she said yes along with everyone else.

"All right." Mr. Roche began to riffle through a stack of papers on his stand. "I'm going to pass out information sheets for you to take home to your parents. You need to get them to sign some medical forms and permission slips. We're going to be having a bake sale and an auction in the next couple weeks. And we need chaperones!"

"My mom hates all this stuff," Sarah said to Lizzie.

"Ask your dad," she said.

"He hates it, too," Sarah said. He didn't, actually, but Sarah didn't like for him to be too involved with her school stuff. Diane was always wanting to volunteer for things. She was a chef. Heading up a bake sale would be just the kind of thing she'd want to do.

Sarah didn't like her volunteering. Diane was always trying to pretend to be her real mom.

"Competing is a lot of work, people!" Mr. Roche said. He had a big smile on his face, as though work were really like spending a day at the beach.

"I knew it," Lizzie said. "Except for flying and staying in a motel, this trip is going to be heinous."

"I know," Sarah said, even though she could tell from her voice that Lizzie was just as excited as everyone else.

"Los Angeles is right next to Hollywood," Marjorie said when Sarah arrived at their palm tree and told her the news. "You're so lucky. You can see Grauman's Chinese Theatre, and the movie studios, and—"

"There isn't going to be time for that," Sarah said. "Not even time for Disneyland. Mr. Roche says all we're doing is singing. We don't even get to go to the beach."

"Who'd want to go to the beach when you could see the Walk of Fame?"

"What's that?"

"In Hollywood, when you get to be famous, you get a star on the sidewalk with your name alongside it. My grandma says it's really fun to walk down the sidewalk and look for your favorite stars."

"I don't think we're going to have time for that, either," Sarah said. "It's going to be singing all the time."

"Do you have to take a bus?"

"No. A plane. Lizzie and I are going to get a window seat and a middle seat and then take turns looking out."

Immediately Sarah felt guilty. For no reason.

"Lizzie Lowitz?" Marjorie pulled her lunch bag out of her backpack and sniffed it. "She seems nice."

"She is nice. Really nice. In fact," Sarah said, her heart thumping, "I was thinking maybe we could all eat together sometime."

Marjorie nodded. "Who does she eat with?"

"Carly Breslow, I think." Sarah didn't know Carly very well. In third grade, she'd been the first person to get a glow-in-the-dark retainer. "You want to find them now?"

"Sure," Marjorie said.

It hurt Sarah's heart a little, how much she loved Marjorie, how Marjorie was always ready to be friendly to new people, how she didn't mind that Lizzie and Sarah had plans to sit together on the airplane. Sarah tried to imagine how it would make her feel if Marjorie had another friend. She thought she might be jealous. She would still want Marjorie to like her best.

Slowly they toured the schoolyard, passing all the kids clumped together in their own groups. Some kids were eating; others were playing basketball. The sun was exactly overhead. In the distance, the hills were brown and gray, like old wood you found at the beach. It wasn't the way it was in books, where the leaves turned red and orange and gold. A lot of trees in California stayed green all year. Still, you knew it was fall. The air smelled warm and smoky. All the classrooms had pumpkins on the doors.

It was hard to find anyone in particular, but suddenly Sarah saw them. Lizzie and Carly were sitting on the ground in front of Mr. Mayberry's room, with their backs against the building right next to the classroom door.

"There they are," she said.

At the same moment, Lizzie looked their way.

"Hey, Sarah!" she said.

It made Sarah brave. She walked closer.

"Can we sit with you guys?" she asked.

In middle school, Sarah knew, you couldn't just sit wherever you wanted. You had to ask.

"Sure," Lizzie said.

Carly said nothing, but she was eyeing Marjorie with caution.

Sarah sat across from them on the walkway. Marjorie lowered herself next to Sarah but didn't actually sit.

"Hey, Carly," Sarah said.

"Hey." Carly was now looking at Marjorie with frank distaste. Sarah knew her mom would say to introduce them, but that would have been weird. She kept her mouth shut and, in her head, she ordered Marjorie to sit down like a normal person.

"Why are you guys over here?" Lizzie asked.

"We just thought it would be fun," Sarah said. "It's boring on our bench."

Lizzie nodded happily. "We've been trying to figure out the cutest guy in French," she said. She added, "All the really cute guys take Spanish."

"I take Spanish," Sarah said. "No one is cute at all."

Except Robert Whitchurch, she thought, but didn't say. Robert was also in chorus. Sarah wasn't ready for Lizzie to know that she thought he was cute.

"I think Cameron Cruz is cute, except for his tight pants," Lizzie said. "But Carly says Everett diCreszenza is cuter."

"Yeah, because he's so tall," Sarah said, smiling at Carly, not wanting her to think that just by sitting with them, she was trying to steal Lizzie away from her.

But Carly was still staring at Marjorie, who was peeling her banana.

"Marjorie," she said, "why are you squatting like that?"

Marjorie took a bite of her banana and then, her mouth still full, said, "I'm a little gassy."

Sarah felt the blood stop moving in her veins.

"Gross!" Carly's face crinkled up in disgust.

"Marjorie!" Sarah couldn't help it.

"What?" As usual, Marjorie was completely clueless.

"Farting is heinous," Lizzie said. "If you're going to be farting, you have to sit somewhere else."

"Well—" Marjorie began.

"You guys!" Sarah hissed. She knew she had to do something. "Quit talking about farting! Steve Birgantee is looking over here!"

Steve Birgantee was the most popular boy in the seventh grade. He was tall and played every sport. Also, unlike Alison Mulvaney, he seemed genuinely nice. People really liked him.

"Oh, God!" Lizzie said, sighing. "Isn't he amazing?"

"I love how his arms are all veiny," Carly breathed.

"And how he looks tan, but not like he's *trying* to look tan," Lizzie said. "You know what I mean?"

Marjorie opened her mouth, but before she could say no, Sarah said, "Exactly." Actually, she had no idea what Lizzie was talking about, but she knew enough to know that when you were trying to make new friends, you had to pretend to understand everything they said. But Marjorie, she was sure, would have no idea. The best thing to do was to make sure Marjorie never got a chance to say anything at all.

Carly tossed her balled-up lunch bag into a nearby trash can.

She groaned. "I hate having science right after lunch," she said. "Mayberry talks about molds and fungi, and I almost throw up. What time is it, anyway?"

Before Sarah could stop her, Marjorie said, "One twenty-three." She said it with an English accent, with her head held up high, as though she were introducing an opera singer to an auditorium full of people in fancy evening clothes.

"How do you know?" Carly asked. "You don't even have a watch."

"I can just tell," Marjorie said in her regular voice. "I have an internal clock in my brain. It's one of my gifts."

"What do you mean, 'gifts'?" Lizzie asked. She sounded skeptical.

"My mom says it's just one of those things I can do that other people can't. It's almost magical, she says." Marjorie seemed to like that Carly and Lizzie were paying so much attention to her.

Lizzie glanced at her cell phone, which was on, even though it wasn't supposed to be. Sarah marveled at her nerve. The principal confiscated cell phones if they rang during school hours.

"It *is* one twenty-three," she said.

"It's like I'm a robot and I was programmed to always know what time it is," Marjorie said.

"What are you talking about?" Carly said. "Why do you even want to *be* a robot?"

Sarah closed her eyes. She knew what was coming.

"It is one twenty-three," Marjorie said in a staccato, robotic voice. "Now it is one twenty-four." She stood up, held out her arms stiffly, and tilted forward from the waist, then stood up straight. "Warning, Will Robinson! It is one twenty-four. Warning! Warning!"

Lizzie whispered, "Why is she doing that?"

"It's from an old TV show. *Lost in Space*," Sarah said miserably. "It's in black-and-white. There's a robot in it."

"Make her stop!" Carly whispered.

Fortunately, at that moment the bell rang. At one twenty-five exactly, as Sarah was sure Marjorie already knew from her magic brain clock.

On the way back to class, Sarah said, "Why did you talk about farting?"

"I didn't say anything about farting. I said I was gassy."

"It's the same thing!" She took a breath and dodged a clot of eighth grade boys. "Marjorie, just for your information, don't talk about farting with new people. Ever. I mean, don't even say anything that has anything to *do* with farting."

"Why? Everybody gets gas."

"*Because!* It's gross. People like talking about nice things when you don't know them very well."

"I wasn't really talking about farting. I was just answering a question."

"And don't pretend to be a robot. Or somebody British. Or anybody with a funny voice." Without waiting for her to ask why, Sarah said, "It makes people feel uncomfortable when they don't know what you're talking about."

"But—"

"I'll see you later," she said, turning down a less-crowded hallway.

Marjorie was driving her insane.

And she wasn't too thrilled with herself, either.

CHAPTER 4

THEY STARTED EATING with Lizzie and Carly every day. Sarah always asked Marjorie if she minded, and she always said no. Still, Sarah wasn't sure Marjorie was too happy about it. She didn't say much. When they talked about boys, which was most of the time, Marjorie stared out at the playground or rummaged around in her lunch bag.

After a few days, Sarah was kind of sick of talking about boys, too. She wasn't exactly sure what Lizzie and Carly meant by "cute." Sometimes it was a boy with a really good tan. Sometimes it was a boy who wore expensive sneakers. Sometimes it was a boy who looked like a famous movie star. A famous *young* movie star. When Marjorie said that a boy in her English class looked like Humphrey Bogart, Lizzie and Carly had no idea what she was talking about. When Marjorie explained, Carly rolled her eyes.

Still, even if she didn't always know what they meant, Sarah liked being in on the conversations. It was nice to be talking about things that she read about in teen magazines: boys and clothes and hairstyles. Carly wanted to be a makeup artist at the mall when she grew up. She told Sarah that sometime she'd show her how to put on eyeliner so that it would make her eyes look smoky.

"I don't think my mom would like that," Sarah said.

"We can do it before school, and you can wash it off before you go home," Carly said.

"That's what I do," Lizzie said. "My mom is so bizarre."

That was another thing they talked about: how their mothers were weird and old-fashioned and irritating, how they didn't understand anything, how they tried to control their children's lives. To Sarah, it was a relief to have friends who knew about this. Marjorie still thought everything about her parents was perfect.

On one of their after-school trips to the Juice Warehouse, Sarah was amazed to find out that Lizzie's parents were divorced, too.

"Since I was in kindergarten," Lizzie said. "I can barely remember what it was like when we all lived in the same house."

"Is your dad remarried?" Sarah asked.

Lizzie nodded. "My mom, too. To *Doug*." She said "Doug" the way other people said "earwax." "Actually, he's not so bad. He's kind of cool, actually. He's a lawyer. He makes tons of money."

"My mom would probably like to marry a lawyer," Sarah said, although she couldn't imagine her being married to anyone.

"Now, my stepmom, on the other hand, is totally heinous," Lizzie said. "Bunny. Bunny Lowitz. Can you even believe that's her name?"

"What do you hate about her?"

"Everything," Lizzie said, sucking the last of her orange-kiwi smoothie into the straw. "She cleans my room without asking just so she can look in my drawers and go through my wastebasket. She buys me bras. To bond with me, she says."

"Gross."

"I throw them away. In the dumpster behind the school, so she doesn't find out." Lizzie sighed heavily. "She always tries to have talks with me about sex and drugs. 'Tell me what all the kids are saying,'" Lizzie said, changing her voice to sound shrill and scratchy at the same time.

"My stepmother collects dolls," Sarah said.

"What kind of dolls?"

"Those big ones with googly eyes and ringlets. They're dressed to look like southern belles and queens and Shirley Temple. No matter where you are in my dad's house, there's a doll on a shelf looking at you. It's so creepy."

Lizzie shook her head. "Beyond creepy," she said.

"What is wrong with people?" Sarah asked. "Especially stepmothers."

It felt so good to talk about it with someone who really understood. Marjorie knew that Sarah hated Diane. Marjorie always tried to make her feel better, which Sarah appreciated, but it wasn't the same as talking to Lizzie, who really *knew*.

"Speaking of something being wrong with people," Lizzie said, "what is wrong with Marjorie?"

Sarah felt herself tense up. "What do you mean, what's wrong with her?" she asked.

Lizzie put her hand on Sarah's arm. "Don't worry. I'm not going to say she can't eat with us anymore. I know she's your best friend."

Sarah's muscles unclenched in relief.

"But she *is* weird," Lizzie said.

"I know."

"I mean, the stuff she eats. And the way she doesn't even care about her clothes or the way she looks."

"She does care," Sarah said, wanting to be loyal but

also wanting to let Lizzie know that she knew what she meant. "She just has different taste from everybody else."

"Doesn't she get that no one else wears clogs?"

"She doesn't care about what other people do," Sarah said. "She's an individualist." She felt proud saying it. Marjorie really wasn't like anyone else.

"Well, boys don't like it if you're an individualist. Unless you have a tattoo," Lizzie said. "They might like that."

"I don't think Marjorie has a tattoo."

"She should get one," Lizzie said, throwing her Styrofoam cup into the trash can. "It might help."

They walked through the parking lot. The supermarket was having a sale on pumpkins; lots of moms were hoisting them into the backs of their SUVs. For the first time in months, the sky was cloudy. Sarah had heard on the news that it might rain on Halloween. It made her sad for the little kids, who got only one chance a year to trick-or-treat.

She wasn't sure about trick-or-treating for herself. She still wanted to do what she had done every year: dress up and go door-to-door with Marjorie, then go back to the Fingerhuts' for hot chocolate and five pieces of candy. Just five, Marjorie's mom would say, and then leave the room so they could cheat and eat more.

But she was pretty sure she was too old to do that this year.

"You know," Sarah said as she and Lizzie stood at the curb, waiting for the light to change. "I'm not sure if she's my best friend anymore."

It shocked her when she said it. The minute the words were out of her mouth, she knew they were true.

"She's my *oldest* friend," she said.

"Well, who's your best friend, then?" Lizzie asked.

Sarah was too shy to say that Lizzie was, maybe.

"Maybe I'm just one of those people who doesn't have a best friend," she said. "Who has a few really good friends."

Lizzie watched the cars gridlock in front of them.

"Carly's my best friend because we live on the same street and eat lunch together every day," she said. "Rachel Zeigler's my second-best friend. She goes to my temple. You're my third-best friend."

"Really?" Sarah said, feeling flattered.

"It might change after the trip," she said. "Rachel's chewing really gets on my nerves."

The light finally changed. As they crossed the street, Sarah wondered if Alison Mulvaney would still think she was a loser if she knew that Sarah was Lizzie's third-best friend and gaining.

* * *

That evening, after homework, Sarah was lying on her bed when her mom knocked on the door.

"What are you reading?" she asked, making room for herself on the bed.

Sarah showed her. It was a book written by a nurse about her experience in the Gulf War.

"Pretty grim reading," Mom said.

"It's not so bad," Sarah said. "I like the part where she talks about how she helped the soldiers."

"Doctors help just as much as nurses," Mom said. "Maybe you should think about being a doctor."

"They help in different ways," Sarah said. "I like the way nurses help more."

It was an ongoing battle. Sarah didn't expect to convince her.

Mom looked around. "This room could use a little dusting," she said.

She was always offering to tidy up Sarah's room. Sarah liked it just the way it was: the bookshelves full of all the chapter books she'd ever owned, and even some of her favorite picture books that she couldn't bring herself to give away, her bed up against the wall under a poster of penguins on a glacier. Her desk, which was kind of beat up from all the pen marks and nicks and scratches on it, sat under the window, where she could look out and see the street three floors down. It wasn't much of a view—just the sidewalk and other apartment buildings that looked almost the same—but she liked it anyway.

"I'll do it later," Sarah said.

"You always say that, and you never do."

Her room at Dad's was full of new furniture and carpeting, and always clean. She had tried putting a poster on the wall, but Diane said she didn't want holes in the new paint, so Sarah had to take it down. It didn't feel like a real room. It felt like a motel. Sarah was glad she had to go over there only one weekend a month and for dinner once a week.

"A little dust isn't going to hurt me," she said. "I read somewhere that kids whose rooms are dusty have less asthma than kids whose rooms are really clean."

"Where did you read that?"

"Some book. I forget."

"When I was your age, I liked *Forever* and *He's My Baby Now*. Don't you ever read books like that?"

"Sometimes."

Mom reached out and gently pushed the hair off Sarah's forehead. "You can't save people, you know," she said.

"What about all the kids you teach?" Sarah asked. "You help them."

"Helping isn't saving," Mom said.

Sarah moved her head away from Mom's hand. "Well, I think you can do both. Sometimes," she said.

"You're a very sweet girl," Mom said.

Sarah thought Mom might cry. "If I promise to dust, will you stop saying things like that?" she asked.

Mom laughed. "Don't promise. Do it. Promises don't mean anything," she said, standing up and backing toward the door.

"All right, all right." But inside Sarah felt sad, because she knew that was what her mother really thought.

She resented the way her mother seemed to think that she never kept her promises. She kept promises all the time. She filled Henry's water dish whenever it was empty. She turned off lamps whenever she left a room. She did her homework without fail.

The thing was, there were different kinds of promises. The kind you wanted to keep—the easy kind—and the kind you didn't. The kind that made you feel terrible when you broke them, and the kind that made you feel terrible when you kept them. Those were the worst: the promises you were stuck with.

There should be extra credit, like on a test, for keeping those, she decided.

* * *

After dinner, Marjorie called.

"You have to come over and get fitted for your space-alien costume," she said.

Sarah had almost forgotten about Marjorie's space-alien movie. Also, she realized that she hadn't been over to her house for a while. She kept canceling to make time for going to the Juice Warehouse with Lizzie.

"Okay. When?" she asked, promising herself that she would go whenever Marjorie said.

And promising herself to keep her promise.

"Louellen is coming home for fall break on Wednesday," Marjorie said. "Come on Thursday. You can stay for dinner."

Sarah loved dinner at the Fingerhuts'. Mr. Fingerhut usually cooked. He liked serving food from foreign countries that no one knew about, like Mongolia and Finland. And he didn't care if you didn't eat something that looked gross. He made squid once, and when Sarah told him she didn't want any, he laughed and didn't say anything about just trying it.

"Joey and I are halfway finished with the script," Marjorie said. "Maybe we can do a read-through."

Sarah still had no idea who Joey Hooper was. She had asked Marjorie to point him out at lunch, but Marjorie always said she couldn't find him.

Sarah had a feeling Joey Hooper ate out by the soccer field.

"Come at four," Marjorie said. "And be prepared. Louellen uses lots of pins."

Great, Sarah thought. Now I get to be weird in public *and* get stuck with pins.

"We have a title, though." Marjorie paused. "Don't you want to know what it is?"

"Sure," Sarah said, sighing. She knew Marjorie could tell from the way her voice sounded how little she cared. But she couldn't seem to manage to sound excited.

She wished she'd never agreed to be in Marjorie's weird movie.

"*Middle School Space Alien,*" Marjorie said. "Doesn't that have a great ring to it?"

"I guess."

"That way, if there are sequels, they can be *Attack of the Middle School Space Alien!* or *Middle School Space Alien Rides Again!*"

"Wouldn't that be for a cowboy movie? Like, if the space alien was riding a horse?"

"You can ride a spaceship," Marjorie said defensively.

Sarah sighed. Even her movie titles were weird.

"You never know," Marjorie said.

She sounded like Sarah's mom. Sarah felt irritation surge in her veins. "And anyway, why are you talking about a sequel?" she asked crankily. "I never said I'd do a sequel."

"Directors have to think like that," Marjorie said. "I probably won't do one, actually. Next semester we have to make documentaries."

Immediately Sarah felt sorry. "I *might* be in a sequel," she said. "If I have time."

She hoped Marjorie believed it: that the only reason she didn't want to do a sequel was because she was busy.

She hoped so, but she was pretty sure Marjorie knew she was lying.

Marjorie always knew.

CHAPTER 5

"HOLD STILL!" Louellen said grumpily. She knelt at Sarah's feet, fiddling with the hem of her costume. A red cushion wrapped around her wrist was full of pins.

They were in Marjorie's room, on the second floor of the Fingerhuts' house, under the eaves. Sarah guessed that no one had cleaned it since Marjorie was a baby. There were clothes all over the floor, even things that didn't fit anymore, things she hadn't worn in a year. There was no desk: Marjorie liked to do homework on her bed. Mrs. Fingerhut (who always insisted that Sarah call her Roxie) said she didn't care as long as Marjorie's grades were good, and she had moved the old desk out. In its place was an ugly green metal filing cabinet, where

Marjorie kept her DVDs. She had so many that the cabinet was full. There were at least ten stacked on top.

The walls were covered with movie posters. You couldn't even see the walls anymore. There were so many posters that most of them were partly under other posters. Marjorie's grandma sent them to her all the time, not just on birthdays and Christmas. Sarah's favorite was a poster of Walt Disney's Tinkerbell, with all the *Peter Pan* movie information written in French. Marjorie said her grandma found that one on eBay.

Louellen looked critically at the hem of the costume. Under it, Sarah's feet in black rubber flip-flops looked strange to her, like pale, shy sea creatures peeking out from under rocks.

"Marjorie, are you sure you don't want this shorter? Because you want her to be able to walk in it," she said.

From the way they looked, you would never know that Louellen and Marjorie were sisters. Louellen had wispy blond hair and red skin on her face and neck, as though she'd been standing over a hot stove. She always looked frazzled and worried, as if a lot of people were depending on her to get things right and she'd better not screw anything up.

Marjorie was staring at Sarah's feet, too. She had her hands on her hips and seemed to be thinking hard.

"No, it has to be long, because I don't want her feet to show. I think it would look wrong if you could see that an alien has feet. I want it to look like she's all blue, and I want the costume to go to the floor."

"Well, okay, but you don't want her to *trip*," Louellen said.

"And it can't look like a dress," Marjorie said. "Can you make it look like more of a tube?"

"You mean like the alien is a worm?" Louellen asked.

"Maybe it would look good if you made it shorter and I wore blue high-tops," Sarah said. She was a little worried about walking around.

"Yes, a worm! Exactly!" Marjorie said, ignoring Sarah completely. "And then you can make the head covering tighter. So it looks like skin."

"It's hot in this thing," Sarah said, fidgeting.

Louellen looked up at her. "Just a few more minutes," she said. She turned back to Marjorie. "And you still want eyestalks, right?"

"Yes. Four. No, six," Marjorie said. "And they should be different lengths. We can attach them all over her head."

"I was thinking pipe cleaners, but with fabric covering them, so it doesn't look tacky," Louellen said.

They were talking as though Sarah weren't even

there. She didn't mind, really. She noticed how Louellen treated Marjorie as someone who knew what she was talking about. To listen to Louellen, you would think that Marjorie had directed hundreds of movies. You would have no idea that they were just sisters, that Louellen had changed her diapers and had once cried when Marjorie spilled a jar of spaghetti sauce on Louellen's ninth grade geometry homework.

Sarah tried to imagine what it must be like to have sisters, and couldn't. To her, family was always just parents and grandparents.

Trying to think about how different Marjorie's life was from hers made her even hotter.

"Come on, you guys," she moaned. "I'm sweating in here."

Immediately Louellen pulled the costume over her head. It made a silky, whooshing sound over Sarah's ears.

"We don't want you fainting," Louellen said soothingly, like a teacher or a mom, like someone used to being the oldest.

Was Louellen weird? Sarah wondered. It was hard to tell. She didn't talk in funny voices or know everything about old movie stars. She had a boyfriend. She was on her college's badminton team. She sewed all her own clothes, which would be considered very weird in seventh grade but maybe was allowed in college.

Bea, the other sister, was a sophomore in high school. Around the house, she pretty much ignored everyone else, which she had been doing since Sarah had known her. She was on the crew team and was vice president of her class. "Is she popular?" Sarah had asked Marjorie once. Marjorie had shrugged. "I don't know," she said. "I just wish she wouldn't leave her towel on the bathroom floor."

Was weirdness something you were born with, like blue eyes or curly hair? If your sister was popular, wouldn't you be, too? Or was it just an accident that had nothing to do with your family or your looks? Was it something that just *happened?*

Sarah really wanted to figure it out. If you could just turn out weird for no reason, then maybe you could become weird out of the blue.

The idea absolutely terrified her.

At dinner, Roxie set an elegantly engraved envelope next to Marjorie's plate.

"An invitation to Cotillion. I'm sure you got one, too, Sarah," Roxie said. "Oh, you girls will have a blast. Remember how much fun Louellen and Bea had when they did Cotillion?"

"What is it, anyway?" Marjorie asked.

Sarah took another bite of her chicken mole and

tried not to sigh too loudly. She didn't even have older sisters, and she knew what Cotillion was. "A social dance class. Boys and girls get dressed up and learn how to dance with each other. Old-fashioned dances like the fox trot and the waltz." Sarah swallowed. "It's not like a regular class. You don't have to take it if you don't want to."

But to Sarah's utter astonishment, Marjorie had perked up.

"Really?" she asked. "Can we wear costumes?"

"No," Louellen said. "You have to wear dresses and high heels, though."

"I can't walk in high heels," Marjorie said.

"Not *high* high heels," Bea said wearily. "Kitten heels."

Before Marjorie could ask what kitten heels were, Sarah asked, "What do the boys wear?"

"Suits. And hard shoes," Louellen said.

"They end up wearing their fathers' clothes," Roxie said. "They all look adorable."

Mr. Fingerhut shook his head. "Those poor guys," he said. "I cannot think of anything more miserable for a twelve-year-old boy than having to get dressed in a suit and touch a girl."

"They wear suits to school?" Marjorie shrieked.

"No, honey," Roxie said. "Cotillion meets on Tuesday nights for six weeks. In the gym."

Marjorie shoveled a forkful of rice into her mouth. A few grains got stuck in her hair.

"It sounds like fun," she said.

"Really?" Sarah asked. "You're going to do it?"

Marjorie nodded. "I love dressing up," she said.

At school on Monday, everyone was talking about it.

"The only bad part is that you have to get assigned to different boys," Lizzie said at lunch. "So if the teacher says you have to dance with Jason Webb, then you have to. You can't say no."

"Who's the teacher?" Sarah asked.

"Mrs. Gretch," Carly said.

"Mrs. Gretch?" Marjorie and Sarah said together, then both burst out laughing.

"What's so funny?" Carly asked suspiciously.

"Have you ever seen her in the parking lot at lunch?" Marjorie asked.

"No," Carly said. "I have better things to do than spy on the teachers at lunch."

"We weren't spying on her," Sarah said, angry on Marjorie's behalf. Carly wouldn't have said that if Sarah had asked the question. "We just saw her one day. She got in her car and sat there smoking, with the windows closed. I think she smoked ten cigarettes."

"Two," Marjorie said. "She smoked two."

"And the whole car filled up with smoke," Sarah said, irritated, because ten cigarettes made it a better story. "We couldn't believe she could even breathe in there. That there was even any oxygen left."

"She's not supposed to smoke at school," Marjorie said.

Lizzie laughed. "I had to go into her room once and borrow some pencils for Mr. Zedaker," she said. "Her breath is heinous."

"From the cigarettes, I bet," Sarah said.

They all laughed. Sarah thought it was the first time since they'd been having lunch together that they'd all laughed at the same time over the same thing. Maybe, she thought, things were looking up.

"What are you going to wear?" Carly asked. Without waiting for an answer, she said, "My mother is going to get me a little black dress, because that's what you should always have in your closet for emergencies."

"What kind of emergencies?" Marjorie asked.

"Like, if you have to go to a party and you have nothing else to wear," Carly explained. "You can wear a little black dress anywhere."

She had read this in one of her magazines, Sarah knew, but she envied the way Carly said it, as if she had been in just this kind of situation, as if she really had emergencies that could be fixed with a dress.

"My mom says I have to wear my black skirt and my red top." Lizzie took a sip from her mini-can of soda. "She says she just bought them a month ago, and that she's not made of money. My mom is so heinously cheap it isn't even funny."

"I'm going to use the money I've been saving since my birthday to buy a new outfit," Sarah said. "Maybe new shoes, too. The shoes I have to wear for chorus are too flat."

"Get a little black dress," Carly said. "But don't let your mom talk you into one that's too long. It has to be short and sexy."

"Sexy?" Marjorie said. "We're *twelve*."

For once, Sarah agreed with her. She could handle cute, but she wasn't ready for sexy.

"What are *you* wearing? Stretch pants and a T-shirt?" Carly asked Marjorie.

"No," Marjorie said. She smiled in a way that Sarah knew she thought was mysterious but really just made her look cross-eyed.

"I don't believe it," Carly said. "That's what you always wear."

"No, really. I'm wearing something else," Marjorie said. "Something special."

"Oh, great," Carly said. "Look, Marjorie. Don't

wear anything strange. Like, your mom's wedding dress or something with feathers. Really. Don't do it."

For once, she sounded to Sarah as though she was genuinely worried about Marjorie. She wasn't being mean. She was trying to get through to her for her own good.

But Marjorie didn't seem to notice. "Nobody else will be wearing anything like it," she said, as though she expected there to be a contest for who was best dressed, and this fact alone was enough to assure her that she was going to win.

"*That* I believe," Carly said.

After school, Marjorie caught up with Sarah as they headed to the parking lot.

"I have to give you your script!" she said, thrusting a sheaf of crumpled computer paper into Sarah's hands. "I finished it last night. It's so good! I can't wait for you to read it and tell me what you think."

"It's pretty long," Sarah said. "How long until I have to have all this memorized?"

"Can you do it by Saturday?"

"That's only five days away!"

"You don't have that many lines," Marjorie said. "Joey has to say more lines than you."

Sarah had to admit that getting to meet Joey Hooper was part of the reason she was still even slightly interested in being in Marjorie's movie. She really wanted to see what kind of boy would work on a project with Marjorie without asking the teacher to move him to another group.

"You mainly just grunt and squeak a lot," Marjorie said.

"Well, I have to know when to grunt and squeak," Sarah said, scanning the parking lot for Mom's beat-up Subaru station wagon. "And I have chorus practice on Wednesday, Thursday, and Friday after school. And Cotillion on Tuesday nights. And homework." Just thinking about everything she had to do made her a little sick. "I need more time."

"Well, not too much more time," Marjorie said. "It's almost Thanksgiving."

Actually, it was still the beginning of November. Halloween had come and gone. Marjorie had mentioned something about trick-or-treating, but Sarah decided that she was too old for pretending to be scared of ghosts and playing along with Roxie's five-pieces-of-candy rule. On Halloween she was at her mom's. They never got any trick-or-treaters there, because kids didn't go to apartments, only houses. Mom put out the plastic pumpkin with the light bulb inside to remind

Sarah of Halloweens when she was a kid, but it just made Sarah sad. After dinner she went into her room and stood at the window watching little bands of dressed-up kids and their parents walk down the sidewalk, heading over to the part of town where the houses were. She was glad for them that it wasn't raining.

Now, though, the clouds were thickening in the sky over the parking lot. A few drops of rain spattered on the cement sidewalk. A flock of seagulls was circling the schoolyard. They were at least thirty miles from the ocean. Grandpa always said the seagulls were a sure sign that a storm was coming. Sarah wished her mom would hurry before she got completely drenched.

"I need at least another week," she said. "I can't even read this until tomorrow. I have too much math."

"Here," Marjorie said, grabbing the script from her hands and turning her around. She unzipped Sarah's backpack. "Put it in here so it doesn't get wet."

Sarah could tell that it was really important to her.

"I'll try to look at it tonight," she said. One of the moms had double-parked her SUV and run into the school office. A bunch of cars behind her were honking. It was giving Sarah a headache.

"Maybe we could just do a walk-through on Saturday," Marjorie said.

"No. I have too much to do. I already said."

"I won't film anything. I just want to see——"

"Marjorie!" Sarah said, shouting a little to be heard over all the horns. "Stop being so pushy!"

Marjorie smiled, the way she always did when someone said something mean to her. But in the split second before she smiled, she looked shocked, as though Sarah had thrown cold water on her or slapped her cheek.

It was just a split second. But Sarah saw it.

"Sorry," she said. "I have a headache."

"That's okay," Marjorie said.

"I always get them in the rain after school," Sarah said. "Especially when all the moms are honking."

"Me, too," Marjorie said, still smiling, but looking a little vague, as though she were really paying attention to something else.

Finally Sarah saw her mom.

"I'll call you tonight," she said, adjusting her backpack on her shoulders and pulling her hoodie over her hair.

She didn't know what made her look back at Marjorie just as she was shoving her backpack into the back seat of Mom's car.

Marjorie was still smiling. But because she stood alone, not talking to anyone in the vast throng of kids waiting for rides, she looked sadder than Sarah had ever seen her.

CHAPTER 6

THAT NIGHT, Grandpa arrived carrying pages of Internet printouts.

"We've got work to do," he said to Sarah, giving Henry a cursory pat on the head.

"What kind of work?" she asked happily. When Grandpa said "work," he meant something fun.

Grandpa set the papers on the coffee table.

"We need some cardboard boxes. Boxes we can cut up. You got any of those?"

"In my closet."

Mom came out of the kitchen, drying her hands on a dishtowel. "I assume this is work that is going to involve an enormous mess," she said.

"We'll clean up," Grandpa said. "Go get those boxes, sweetheart."

When Sarah returned with the boxes, Mom was studying Grandpa's printouts.

"Your grandfather," she said, "is planning on giving Henry an IQ test."

"Standard poodles are very smart," he said. "They're the Einsteins of the dog world."

"I didn't think they were *that* smart." Sarah looked at Henry, who was rubbing his head against the side of the couch as though scratching an itch.

"That's what everyone says," Grandpa said. "The only dogs that are smarter are Border collies."

"Which are the dumbest?" Sarah asked.

"Afghans. They're airheads."

"I don't see how you can tell."

"Well, it's like IQ tests for people. They're not foolproof, but you test their problem-solving skills." Grandpa looked over at Henry, who was still scratching. "I have a feeling ole Henry is going to ace these tests."

"What are the boxes for?" Sarah asked.

"We have to make a barrier. Something he can't see over. We need scissors and tape." Grandpa consulted his notes. "And an old blanket. And some buckets. And some dog treats."

An hour later, they'd set everything up. Sarah and her mom stood behind Grandpa's chair, waiting while he read the instructions one more time. Henry stood beside them, watching them all alertly, seeming to sense that he might be called on to participate in whatever was about to happen.

"Okay," Grandpa said. "Sarah, you got the blanket?"

"Got it."

Grandpa snapped his fingers so that Henry would stand in front of him.

"Henry, sit," he said.

Proud to obey, Henry lowered his haunches to the floor.

"Okay, sweetheart, put the blanket over his head. Gently, so he doesn't panic." Grandpa checked his watch. "We're going to see how long it takes him to shake it off."

Sarah put the gray flannel blanket over Henry's head.

"Don't they put blankets over birdcages so parrots will think it's nighttime?" she asked.

"Shhh," Grandpa said, not taking his eyes off his watch.

Henry stood up immediately. He shook his head, but the blanket still hung over his eyes. He fidgeted some more, dipping his head, and the blanket fell away.

"Nine seconds!" Grandpa bent forward to rub Henry's ear. "Attaboy!"

"Is that good?" Mom asked.

"Under fifteen seconds, and he gets three points. Write that down," he said.

Mom shook her head as she wrote. "I'm having trouble imagining what kind of dog takes longer than fifteen seconds to do that," she said.

Sarah laughed.

"Henry, you ready for your next test?" Grandpa asked.

The dog, leaning hard against Grandpa's hand, did not look ready to stop being scratched.

Grandpa took his hand away.

"Okay, buddy. Okay, now. Time for more work. You ready, Henry?" To Sarah he said, "Sweetheart, let him see you put a treat under one of the buckets."

Sarah held up a bone-shaped doggy cookie for Henry to see. "Now watch, Henry," she said, walking to the far end of the living room, where she'd arranged three overturned plastic sand pails. "See what I'm doing?" She slid the treat under the middle pail.

Henry watched with interest. If Grandpa hadn't been holding him by the collar, he would have padded over to the buckets to have a closer look.

Sarah went to Henry and took him by the collar.

"Turn him around. So his back is to the buckets," Grandpa said.

Sarah made him sit. When he'd stayed put for a few seconds, she said, "Okay," and he rose and went over to the pails. He sniffed at the ground in front of all three, then managed with his nose and right paw to overturn the middle pail and free the treat, which he gobbled with relish.

"Right on the first try!" Grandpa said. "Three more points, Henry!"

Mom wrote it down. "Not bad for a dog who eats empty garbage bags," she said.

"That was only that one time," Sarah said.

"Once was enough," Mom said, shaking her head. "The vet bill was over six hundred dollars."

Henry swallowed his cookie. He seemed pleased to realize he was the kind of dog someone would spend a lot of money to help.

"Okay, Sarah, we need another treat." Grandpa leaned forward and pointed. "Put it right there, under the coffee table. Where he can only reach it with his paw."

The coffee table was low to the ground. Henry cocked his head as Sarah positioned the cookie.

"If he can get the treat with just his paw, he gets another three points," Grandpa said. "No fair using his snout."

Henry paused for only a moment in front of the table. Then he extended his big, curly-haired paw toward the treat. He did it with surprising delicacy, as though a careless move might cause the cookie to fall into a hole in the floor and disappear forever.

When he had maneuvered the cookie out from under the table, and bent to eat it, Sarah, Grandpa, and Mom all cheered at once.

Grandpa pumped a fist in the air. "Seems to me we got us an Einstein here," he said.

"Let's not get carried away," Mom said.

"Paula, I'm telling you, this dog's a gem!" Grandpa turned to Sarah. "Now let's see if he can figure out how to get a treat when it's behind all those cardboard boxes we cut up."

They had flattened a couple of boxes to create a surface about five feet long and three feet tall. Then Sarah had cut a square hole out of the center so that Henry could see through it. They had balanced the whole thing against two more boxes, creating a kind of wall. Sarah set a cookie on the opposite side of the wall, making sure that Henry—Grandpa's hand holding him firmly by the collar—was watching through the makeshift window.

"Okay, buddy," Grandpa said, releasing him. "Show your stuff."

Henry seemed momentarily confused. He moved

toward the cardboard barrier, then sniffed. Cautiously he tried to insert his nose into the cut-out hole.

"Uh-oh," Sarah whispered.

After a moment Henry withdrew his nose. He cocked his head. His tail, wagging almost incessantly, slowed to a stop.

"Come on, buddy," Grandpa said. "You can do it."

Encouraged, Henry stood still for another few seconds. Sarah could almost see him pondering, weighing his options.

Finally, sniffing the air as though it were providing him with invisible clues, he jogged around the barrier and made his way to the cookie.

"Forty-six seconds," Grandpa said, checking his watch. "Not great, but not bad. Give him two points, Paula."

"Maybe he's getting tired," Sarah said.

"Just one more test. Go get his leash. If he hears it jangling and gets excited without you saying a word, he gets another three points."

Sarah ran into the kitchen and took the leash off the counter, where she'd left it after that morning's walk. Heading into the living room, she saw Henry swallow the last of his cookie, then run to her with a hopeful look in his eyes.

"He knows," she said. "Another three points! What's his score, Mom?"

"Fourteen out of fifteen. Brilliant, according to the experts."

"What'd I tell you? Brilliant!" Grandpa smacked his thigh. Then he positioned his hands on the armrest and struggled to push himself to stand up. "Come on, girls. Let's walk ole Einstein here to the corner and get cones. My treat."

It was almost dark out when they got down to the street. Sarah felt a thrill to be getting ice cream before dinner. She peered at the lit windows on the first floor of her building, imagining the families behind the curtains boiling water, setting tables, counting out knives and forks, the air they breathed smelling cozily of frying onions or simmering spaghetti sauce or meat roasting in a hot oven. It made her feel good to think of all the different things there were to eat, all the different ways there were to be a happy family. No one way. You could eat pot roast or an omelet, use paper napkins or fancy cloth ones, drink milk or water or soda out of a can. You could get ice cream first and go back to the house for broiled salmon and buttered rice. There was no one way.

Just then she became aware of Henry pulling her over to a patch of dirt at the curb. Instead of raising his leg to pee, he squatted slightly and the pee sprayed across the backs of his front legs.

"Henry, you slob!" Grandpa cried. "Pick up your damn leg!"

Ignoring him, but feeling the sensation of something wetting the fur of his legs, Henry bent his head down, trying to take a look. He flinched as his own pee hit him on the snout.

Sarah started to laugh. "He peed on his face!"

"Henry!" Mom said. "Oh, good Lord. Henry!"

"Damn dog!" Grandpa said.

Henry ignored them all. He continued to pee, soaking his front legs thoroughly, as though he knew he had made a fool of himself and the only way to proceed was to pretend that nothing whatsoever was amiss.

By now they were all laughing uncontrollably.

"Brilliant!" Mom said. "I think maybe a Rhodes scholar. Maybe a Nobel Prize winner."

"Damn dog," Grandpa grumbled, shaking his head, laughing in spite of himself. "Henry! Don't they teach you the right way to pee in dog school?"

"He doesn't go to school," Sarah said. She was laughing so hard her stomach hurt.

"Well, sign him up," Grandpa said. "He needs to take remedial peeing. Peeing for dummies. Something."

They laughed all the way to the ice cream shop.

They were still laughing an hour later as they lured Henry into the shower at home and rinsed him off.

"Damn dog," Grandpa muttered again, watching as Sarah ran the washcloth over the backs of Henry's legs.

Sarah smiled. It was funny to think that maybe Henry had done it all on purpose. Maybe, she thought, he could tell that he was being judged, and it had made him want to do something crazy and rebellious, something of which no one would approve. After all, why should he be judged? Why couldn't he just do what he wanted? Why did everything have to be a competition? Just thinking this made her even more gentle with his knotty legs, which now seemed strangely fragile, as though they might break if they were scrubbed too hard.

Henry, seeming to realize that he had at last been understood, did his best to remain absolutely still.

CHAPTER 7

AT SCHOOL ON TUESDAY, everyone was acting different. The boys pretended not to care about Cotillion, but Sarah could tell they were just as nervous and excited as the girls.

In Spanish, before Señora Grunewald got into the room, Jesse Pike said in a loud voice that he was going to eat a raw onion before Cotillion so that his breath would smell.

"That way, no one'll pick me!" he said.

All the boys laughed, as though Jesse Pike had thought of an amazing solution to a complicated problem.

Sarah sneaked a look at Robert Whitchurch. She was pretty sure he was only pretending to laugh, that he knew it was stupid.

"Mrs. Gretch will just make some girl dance with you, then," Melinda Bookman said.

"What if he picks his nose?" Rupert Winslow asked.

"And eats it!" Carl Estes yelled.

The boys all dissolved in laughter and shouted about what a good idea this was. The girls all looked disgusted.

"Mrs. Gretch is the assistant principal, not just the special skills teacher," Melinda said. "If she sees you picking your nose and eating it, you're going to get suspended."

"So?" Jesse shrugged. "At least then I don't have to take *dance*."

All the boys seemed to think this was brilliant. They started shouting out other things they could do—farting, throwing up, wearing smelly socks—until Señora Grunewald lumbered into the room.

"Hola," she said, and again, when no one paid any attention, *"HOLA!"*

The class quieted down.

"Let me guess," she said, scanning the room. "Cotillion starts tonight. Right?"

When they all said yes, she sighed and shook her head.

* * *

The gym seemed to light up the rainy night. From Dad's car, it looked cozy and snug, but just knowing that it was going to be full of all the kids she knew, dressed up and waiting for something embarrassing to happen to someone else, made Sarah want to turn around and go home.

"It'll be fun," Dad said. "It's one of those things you hate until you do it, and then you don't hate it anymore."

"I don't think I bought the right shoes," she said. They had looked perfect at the mall, but now, as she was about to get out of the car, she was stricken with doubt.

"They're fine," Diane said. "They're black, and they have the perfect heel. I'll bet you'll be the best-dressed girl there."

Diane always sounded perky and upbeat. Sarah had figured out a long time ago that it wasn't that different from yelling; it was just another way to get people to do what she wanted. Right now, she wanted Sarah to get out of the car so she and Dad could go home and watch basketball.

"Everyone's nervous," Dad said.

"Maybe they already know how to dance," Sarah said. Suddenly it occurred to her that she should have practiced dancing on her own, or at least watched one of Marjorie's old Fred Astaire movies.

"Of course they don't," Diane said. She half turned around so she could look at Sarah face-to-face. Sarah could see the feathery ends of her short dark hair silhouetted against the light shining from inside the gym. "Just laugh if you step on someone's toes. Make a joke out of it."

"What if someone steps on my toes?" Some of those boys were big.

"Laugh at that, too," Dad said. He leaned back and pushed open the car door. "Come on, sweetie. Take the plunge."

"And take that hoodie off when you get inside," Diane said. "It doesn't go with the rest of your outfit."

Sarah pulled the hood over her head and ducked out of the car and into the rain. She thought she might keep the hoodie on. It looked just fine.

The gym was already warm from all the nervous kid bodies. At a table set up just inside the door, a mom was taking names and asking everyone to sign in. "Have a good time!" she sang, handing Sarah a name tag, which she promptly stuffed into the pocket of her hoodie. She thought, I have been going to school with these people for seven years. They already know my name.

The girls stood on one side of the room, giggling and shrieking, pretending that there were no boys around. The boys stood across the room, looking miserable. When they were wearing suits and their fathers' shoes, it was hard to act the way they usually did. A few moms and dads wandered around the room or stood in small groups chatting. They were the chaperones. Mostly they were there in case anyone threw up.

Immediately Sarah found Lizzie and Carly. Lizzie wore a plain black skirt, a red blouse, and black shoes with a wedge heel. Carly wore a black dress and black shoes with pointy toes. They were both wearing a lot of makeup, but it didn't make them look like adults. For some reason, all the kids in the gym looked as though they were playing dress-up.

"You can wear more eye makeup at night," Carly explained. "It says in *Seventeen*."

"My mom would never let me wear all that mascara," Sarah said.

"Mine, neither," Lizzie said. "But Carly's mom doesn't care, so I went over there after school. After this thing is over, I'll go in the bathroom and wash everything off." She looked Sarah up and down. "You look so cute," she said.

"Except for that hoodie," Carly said. "Ditch it."

Sarah pulled it off and tossed it on the floor by the wall, irritated that Diane was right. Without it she felt almost naked, even though she was wearing a dark green turtleneck sweater over a black and green plaid skirt and black nylons.

"You're going to be sweaty," Carly said. "Next time, wear something sleeveless."

"And don't wear stockings," Lizzie said. "My stupid mom tried to get me to wear them."

Sarah nodded, terrified by how many mistakes she had made already. They hadn't even started dancing yet.

"The boys look dumb," Carly said. "Except for Steve Birgantee. He is so unbelievably cute."

"No matter what he's wearing," Lizzie said. "He could be wearing Superman pajamas and still look cute."

"I think Robert Whitchurch looks kind of cute," Sarah ventured shyly.

"Really? Robert?" Lizzie followed her gaze. "I guess he looks better than he usually does in chorus. But his hair is all slicked down."

"Well, yeah," Sarah said, afraid again. "Except for that."

She looked out over the room, trying to find Marjorie. She was pretty sure Marjorie wasn't there, that she would have seen her by now. Sarah missed her. She missed talking about things that didn't have anything to do with boys.

"I can't believe Jason Webb is wearing a bow tie," Lizzie said. "And look how big his shoes are."

"All he needs is a fake red nose, and he'd look like a clown," Carly said.

"I wonder where Alison Mulvaney got that dress," Lizzie said. "I heard her telling Yvonne Brondello that her mom was going to buy her a different dress for each week of dance class."

Carly said something, but Sarah didn't hear what it was. Marjorie had just walked into the gym.

She was wearing a long dress. Not an evening gown, exactly. It was made of beige lace, with long sleeves and a high collar and lots of tiny buttons running up the front. It looked like a Victorian wedding dress. And she wore a hat. Not just any hat: this one was white, with a huge brim and a white scarf that attached to its underside and was tied in a bow beneath her chin.

The room got quiet for just a second, then erupted in sound. The girls were giggling and whispering. The boys were pointing and laughing. Even the chaperones couldn't take their eyes off of her.

"Oh, my God," Lizzie breathed. "What is wrong with her?"

Marjorie walked like a queen into the room, taking slow steps, holding her head high. She wasn't smiling, exactly, but she looked happy to be the center of so much attention. Sarah knew that if anyone started talking to her, she would answer with a British accent.

"She's coming over here!" Carly whispered. "Oh, God, make her go away!"

As Marjorie headed toward them, Sarah could feel her skin burning. She was so angry at Marjorie, for making everyone look, for not caring, for not knowing how to behave.

"You're wearing *gloves?* And *boots?* With *laces?*" Carly hissed when she joined them.

"Marjorie, you cannot dance in boots," Lizzie said. "And you look like Mary Poppins. Or that old English queen who rode around in a carriage."

"My mom won it at a charity winetasting," Marjorie said. "It wasn't even for fancy occasions. Just what ladies wore every day."

"It's, like, four hundred years old!" Carly yelled. "You can't dance in four-hundred-year-old clothes!"

"It's only about a hundred and twenty years old," Marjorie said. She was smiling, but her eyes were crinkled up in a funny way. Did they do this every time she smiled? Why had Sarah never noticed before?

"Ginger Rogers danced in evening gowns," Marjorie said.

"I don't care what your other weird friends do,"

Carly said, "but you can't hang out with us in that thing. You just can't."

"It is pretty heinous," Lizzie said in what Sarah knew was a trying-to-be-gentle voice.

"Ginger Rogers is a movie star," Sarah said.

"What?" Carly stamped her high-heeled foot in frustration. "Sarah! Do you not get that everyone is *staring* at us?"

Sarah got it. "Ginger Rogers isn't a weird friend. She's a movie star," she said.

Mrs. Gretch had moved to the front of the gym. She held a microphone and wore an old-fashioned flowery dress with a matching belt around the middle. Mrs. Gretch was chubby. The belt looked tight.

She tapped on the microphone, then put her mouth too close to it. "Testing, testing," she said.

Marjorie sidled close to Sarah. "She looks like she's going to try to smoke it," she whispered.

Usually this would have made Sarah laugh. But she didn't say a word. She was too angry. And she was sick of defending Marjorie when she did stupid things.

"Will everyone please be quiet?" Mrs. Gretch said.

Jesse Pike pretended to hold a microphone and sing the lyrics to "Seven Nation Army" by the White Stripes. All the boys around him laughed, because it was funny to think of Mrs. Gretch singing in a rock band.

"Boys and girls!" Mrs. Gretch said sternly into the mike. Everyone jumped.

"Hey, not so loud!" Carl Estes yelled, clamping his hands over his ears.

"Attention, please!" Mrs. Gretch said. "I need everyone's attention!"

Finally everyone shut up. Sarah realized her heart was pounding.

"Most of you know me as a teacher and an assistant principal," Mrs. Gretch said, "but what you probably don't know is that I am a ballroom dance aficionado."

Everyone looked confused. A few boys yelled out, "What?"

"I am a fan of ballroom dance," Mrs. Gretch said. "I have been dancing for years. And I like passing on my love of dancing to young people."

She smiled at all of them. From the back of the room, one of the boys belched loudly.

"You all know Mr. Finch?" Mrs. Gretch said, pretending not to hear.

Mr. Finch waved. He was a PE teacher, and his face was bright red from having been hit by lightning. He was wearing a baggy black suit. Usually he wore shorts and a sweatshirt.

"Mr. Finch will be assisting me," Mrs. Gretch said. "And so will our wonderful parents. Let's give our parents a hand."

Everyone clapped dutifully.

"Now," Mrs. Gretch said. "Our first dance is the waltz."

Everyone began to talk again while she turned around and fumbled with the CD player. Lizzie whispered, "Oh, my God, her ass is enormous!" Sarah saw Alison Mulvaney pointing at Marjorie and whispering to Zannie and Yvonne. Marjorie held her head high, as though she were at the opera and trying to see the stage over a tall man in front of her.

Old-fashioned music filled the room.

"Who knows what makes a waltz special?" Mrs. Gretch asked.

Marjorie and a few of the music kids raised their hands, but someone called out, "Three-four time!"

"That's right!" Mrs. Gretch said. She began to rock slowly in time to the music. "Feel the beat. *One*-two-three, *one*-two-three, *one*-two-three, *one*-two-three!"

"This is stupid," Sarah said. "We're never going to have to waltz with anyone."

"You might at a wedding," Carly said. "Or if you ever go to a ball."

"Mr. Finch?" Mrs. Gretch asked into the microphone. "If you would be so kind?"

The kids all stared in embarrassed horror as Mr. Finch and Mrs. Gretch waltzed around at the front of the room. Mr. Finch was young. In his PE classes he let all the kids call him Chuck. Except for having a red face, he was handsome. It was weird to see them holding each other the way Fred Astaire and Ginger Rogers did. It made Sarah realize that you didn't have to be in love to dance.

While they were dancing, one of the moms came up behind Marjorie and put a hand on her shoulder. Sarah heard her whisper, "Let me take your hat, honey. So you won't put somebody's eye out." Marjorie untied her scarf and let the mom take her hat away. Without it, she looked small and sad, like a wet dog.

"All right," Mrs. Gretch said. She was a little out of breath. "Girls, line up on this side of the room. Boys, line up over there."

"This is it," Lizzie hissed. "Try to get across from someone cute."

Sarah could see that everyone else had the same idea. Alison Mulvaney was shoving people to make sure she was across from Steve Birgantee.

Even after they had all achieved a semblance of a line, a few boys kept pushing each other. Sarah could see that they were the boys across from Marjorie, who didn't seem to notice, except for the way one of her eyes was twitching.

Her twitchy eye made Sarah's heart hurt.

"Boys, that's enough!" Mrs. Gretch said sternly. "Now, everyone, approach your partner, please."

Sarah ended up with Dylan Dewitt, who was pretty cute except for having huge teeth.

"Hey," Dylan said. "I hate this. My mom is making me."

"Mine, too," Sarah said, which wasn't true, but she felt she had to say it.

Mrs. Gretch was explaining how they had to hold each other.

"Sorry," Dylan said when he took Sarah's right hand with his left. "I'm not always this sweaty."

"It's okay."

"And I have canker sores. But they're not contagious."

"Are you sure?" she asked. "I think they're from a virus."

"Not these canker sores!" Dylan said proudly.

"Well, okay," she said, even though the idea of touching anyone with canker sores made her want to scrub her hands with a Brillo pad.

Everyone practiced one-two-three-ing while Mrs.

Gretch counted out the beats. The chaperones walked around making sure they were doing it right.

"Very good!" Mrs. Gretch said. "Now with the music!"

While they waited for the waltz to start, Dylan leaned forward.

"What?" Sarah said, backing away, not wanting his canker sores too close.

"What is wrong with your friend?" Dylan whispered.

She glanced over at Marjorie, who was standing straight and tall while a boy Sarah didn't know argued with one of the chaperones. She could tell he was refusing to dance with Marjorie. Finally the chaperone grasped his arm and pulled him toward Marjorie. The boy held his arms the right way, but when Marjorie put her hand in his, he looked away, as if by not looking at her, he could make her disappear.

"I don't know," Sarah said to Dylan as music flooded the room. "That's just how she is."

CHAPTER 8

THE NEXT DAY AT LUNCH, Sarah waited for Marjorie outside her video production class, just as she always did. But when Marjorie came out, she didn't have her backpack.

"I have to skip lunch," she said, leaning against the classroom door to hold it open. "Joey and I have to work on some stuff."

"What stuff?"

"How we want to shoot the movie. The lighting. Camera angles. That kind of thing."

"Wow," Sarah said, impressed. "Will it take long? Because I can wait."

"No, just go eat without me. I don't want to rush," Marjorie said. She seemed eager to go back in the classroom.

"Well, okay," Sarah said. This would be the first time ever that she wasn't eating lunch with Marjorie, except for the few times when one of them had been sick. It seemed weird to eat without her.

"Want me to get you anything?" Sarah asked.

"No. I've got my lunch. I'm going to eat at the computer," Marjorie said. She turned and went back into the classroom. "Thanks, though!" she called out just before the door swung shut.

As she made her way to Lizzie and Carly's spot, Sarah thought how horrible it would be if she didn't have them to eat with. Nothing was worse in middle school than not having someone to eat with. It was a good thing she had some extra friends, she thought, reminding herself of her mother.

Lizzie and Carly couldn't stop talking about Cotillion.

"Alison definitely had the best dress," Carly said. "I can't believe she's only going to wear it once. If I had that dress, I'd wear it every week and be happy."

"It's so unfair. She's got a red iPod *and* a Black-Berry," Lizzie said. "Her parents buy her too much stuff." But she sounded jealous as she said it.

"Didn't you think the boys looked hilarious?" Carly said. "Seeing them in suits just made me realize how gross they really are." She paused. "Except for Steve Birgantee. He looked pretty good."

"They could have taken showers. They could have at least washed their hair." Lizzie shivered as she took a delicate bite of a Nutter Butter, which she was holding the way old ladies held teacups. "Some of them smelled."

"I think it was on purpose," Carly said. "I think they didn't use deodorant so they'd smell and we'd be disgusted. They thought it would be funny."

"Not all of them," Lizzie said. "Some of them are just pigs." She pulled her thick, frizzy hair up into a ponytail, as if she were giving the back of her neck some room to breathe. "The cutest boy I danced with was Jesse Pike," she said, letting her hair fall back down. "He's not really that cute, but he's better than Eugene Brownmueller."

"Both the boys I got were disgusting," Carly said. "And I would have gotten Steve Birgantee the second time if Yvonne Brondello hadn't cut in line. She actually pushed me out of the way to get to him."

"You should have pushed back," Lizzie said.

"Have you seen her arms?" Carly swallowed the last of her cracker. "I'm a little afraid of her."

"Who did you think was best-looking other than Steve Birgantee?" Sarah asked, just to have something to say. She was actually a little bored. She kept wondering what Marjorie was doing. She missed her.

"Maybe Thomas Su. Maybe Nick Ballantine," Lizzie said. "Who did you think was cute?"

"Robert Whitchurch looked kind of okay," Sarah said.

Carly was looking at her fingernails, checking to make sure they were all the same length. "I think he likes you," she said to Sarah. "He kept looking at you."

"He does not like me," Sarah said, but inside, she felt hot and fluttery.

"Well, why was he looking at you, then?" Carly asked.

"If he liked me, he would have tried to get in the right place in line to dance with me," Sarah said.

"Not necessarily," Lizzie said. "Boys are idiots."

"Do you like him?" Carly asked.

Sarah hesitated. She wanted to tell someone that she might like Robert Whitchurch, that she didn't want a boyfriend or anything, but she might like him, maybe. It would be a relief to say it out loud. But telling someone seemed a little dangerous, like going through a door with a NO ENTRANCE sign.

"No," she said. "I mean, I like him. But I don't *like* him."

"You like him," Carly said. "I can tell."

"No, I don't."

"Then why are you blushing?" she asked.

"Because I'm hot," Sarah said. "Quit it."

"Come on," Lizzie said. She took one of Carly's crackers. "Just because you like someone doesn't mean you *like* him."

"Stop stealing my food," Carly said. She took another look at her nails. "I don't like anyone. Even Steve Birgantee. I mean, he's really cute and really nice, but he's not really my type."

"How can someone cute and nice not be your type?" Lizzie asked.

It was a relief to hear them chatter, to listen and not have to say anything. To not be missing Marjorie anymore. To think, in the privacy of her own head, about how Robert might like her.

In chorus, Mr. Roche handed out updated rehearsal schedules.

"After school every day until six," he said. "And every weekend. Ten to three, Saturdays and Sundays."

"That's like two extra days of school!" Nina French wailed. "I have to go to church!"

"There will be exceptions for religious services," Mr. Roche said. "But not for anything else. This is serious, people. Commitment!"

"How are we even supposed to do homework?" Robert Whitchurch whispered to Sarah.

"Or do anything?" Sarah whispered back.

That was when she remembered Marjorie's movie.

"We have two and a half weeks. Two and a half weeks!" Mr. Roche said. "We have to use all the time we have left to prepare."

Sarah raised her hand. "But Mr. Roche—"

"No buts!" he boomed. "I told you all that this was how it had to be if you want to win the competition. Chorus comes first."

"But—"

He glared at her.

"No exceptions," he said.

Sarah lowered her hand. She knew it was pointless to argue. She sagged in her seat, washed over by foreboding, knowing what she was going to have to do.

"I can't believe I have to miss basketball tryouts," Robert said.

"That's too bad," she said, trying not to notice Lizzie making faces at her, which was just Lizzie's way of saying how cool it was that Robert was talking to her.

"What do you have to miss?" he asked.

"Nothing as big as that," she said.

She told Marjorie that afternoon in the parking lot while Marjorie waited to be picked up.

"I can do it after three o'clock on weekends," she

said, shouting a little to be heard over all the kids who were waiting for rides home.

"That won't work," Marjorie said. "I need daylight. It's almost dark by four now. We won't have enough time."

"We could do it in the morning. I could get up early."

"There still wouldn't be enough time," Marjorie said, pushing her glasses up her nose.

It was cold and windy; overhead, smoke-colored clouds raced across the last of the blue sky. Sarah wore a hoodie and a sweatshirt, but she shivered anyway.

"It's probably going to be raining anyway. Maybe we could film it inside."

Marjorie smiled. "It's okay," she said. "I'll just get someone else to do it."

"Who?"

Marjorie pushed at her glasses again. Sarah realized that even though she was still smiling, she was looking away.

"Joey, or maybe Bea, if she's around. Don't worry about it. I'll find someone."

"Marjorie," Sarah said, "I'm really sorry."

"Don't worry about it." She was looking out over the parking lot.

"I don't want to mess up your project."

Marjorie looked right at her. She wasn't smiling anymore. "It's not a big deal," she said.

"Marjorie—"

"I *said* don't worry about it!" she yelled, pushing past her.

"Marjorie!" Sarah tried to grab her backpack, but Marjorie had already stepped up to the curb. She looked left and right, as though maybe if she just looked harder, her dad's car would magically appear.

Sarah thought about following her and apologizing some more. But she didn't. She just watched as Marjorie stood there, hair blowing messily around her head, a too-small orange ski jacket pulled off her shoulders by her heavy backpack. Her flared jeans were too short, and she was wearing white gym socks with her black suede clogs.

Next to Sarah, two eighth grade boys were laughing.

"Is that the one?" the shorter one asked.

"Yeah. She went to Cotillion in a *wedding* dress," the other one answered. "My brother said."

"Dude! It's the bride of Frankenstein!" The short boy stuck his arms straight out and walked in place without bending his knees. "Dance with me! Dance with me!" he said in a jerky voice that sounded a lot like Marjorie being a robot.

It *wasn't* a wedding dress! Sarah yelled in her head. But she didn't say a word.

That afternoon, Mr. Roche was cranky. They sang "Sing for Joy" for an hour and a half, and he still wasn't satisfied.

"Pretend Handel is in the room listening," he said, blotting his sweaty forehead with his arm. "Would you try harder if Handel was standing here instead of me?"

"Isn't Handel dead?" Jason Webb called out.

"Stop trying to be funny, Jason," Mr. Roche said sternly. "This is serious business."

Lizzie raised her hand. "Mr. Roche, can we please have a break?" she asked. "My throat is getting sore."

Mr. Roche glanced up at the clock. "Ten minutes," he said, slamming his baton onto his music stand.

Lizzie and Sarah ducked into the covered outdoor hallway and ran for the bathroom. Rain was pouring from the sky, dripping from the gutters, puddling on the pavement. The schoolyard was deserted except for a grown-up man jogging around the soccer field in a sodden tracksuit. It was hard even to imagine it on a sunny day, filled with kids.

"I am so sick of singing," Lizzie said as she looked at herself in the mirror.

"Me, too," Sarah said from the stall. "I'm not so sure I even like singing anymore."

"The competition will be cool," Lizzie said. "I heard that afterward there's a party with all the schools. Maybe there will be some cute boys there."

"Where did you hear that?"

"From Nina French's older sister. She went two years ago. Mr. Roche doesn't tell us, because he wants us to think it's all serious work and not any fun."

"I guess that'll be okay," Sarah said, emerging from the stall and turning on the water to wash her hands.

Lizzie pulled her hair off her neck, then let it loose.

"Hey, what's wrong with you?" she asked. "You're acting different."

"No, I'm not." Sarah rubbed her hands together, watching the pink soap powder turn into flimsy, foamy bubbles. "I'm just so mad at Marjorie."

Until the words were out of her mouth, she had thought she was just feeling guilty.

"How come?"

"I'm supposed to be in this movie she's making for video production." She held her hands under the water and watched as the bubbles slid down the drain. "This stupid movie. It's about a space alien."

Lizzie laughed. "That sounds like a movie Marjorie would make," she said.

"I told her I would be free all day this weekend and

the next to film it, and now I can't because of rehearsal. And when I told her, she was nasty about it."

"That's so heinous," Lizzie said.

"I mean, I apologized. I said I would get up early or meet her after rehearsal. I tried to make it right." Sarah pulled a paper towel from the dispenser. She could feel a few granules of soap, gritty like sand, stuck to her skin. "I said I was sorry."

But she knew that she was still breaking a promise and saying she was sorry didn't fix it.

"She should be nice about it," Lizzie said. "It's not your fault."

Sarah threw the paper towel away. "She should be grateful I'd even think about doing it," she said. "It's a *blue* space alien."

"Uh-oh," Lizzie said. "Bad wardrobe alert."

"You should see the stupid costume I was supposed to wear."

"Maybe it's just as well," Lizzie said, giving herself one more look in the mirror.

Sarah flicked off the overhead light.

"I *said* I was sorry," she said.

CHAPTER 9

MARJORIE HAD TO WORK on her movie during lunch every day that week. On Friday, Sarah didn't even go to the video production classroom to see if Marjorie wanted to eat with them. She figured Marjorie knew where to find them.

On Saturday morning, Sarah woke up early. At first she thought it was just a regular Saturday, lazy and long, with nothing to do. Just thinking that made her stretch with happiness. But in the middle of stretching, she remembered.

Mom drove her to school. The sidewalks were wet and the sky was gray, but a few blue patches were showing.

"Is it supposed to rain today?" Sarah asked as they turned into the parking lot.

"Not today," Mom said. "The paper said we're getting a break."

Sarah gazed up at the dark clouds. "Well, it *could* rain," she said.

"Anything's possible," Mom said. "You should have brought an umbrella."

Sarah didn't feel like explaining for the fortieth time that you weren't supposed to carry an umbrella in middle school.

Mom pulled up to the curb. "Everything all right?" she asked.

"Yeah," Sarah said, unbuckling her seat belt. "Don't forget to tell me if Marjorie calls."

"I won't," Mom said, "but isn't that Marjorie over there?"

Sarah looked to where she pointed. Marjorie stood with a much younger boy in the middle of the soccer field. The boy looked as though he was maybe in fourth grade. He was holding a video camera and listening to Marjorie, who was talking loudly and excitedly. She was covered head to toe in the blue space-alien costume. Louellen had sewn an elastic drawstring through the bottom hem so that it was gently cinched. The costume was short enough to walk around in, but long enough to cover Marjorie's shoes. With the hood, she looked like a giant blue hot dog. Except for the eyestalks, which bobbed up and down as she spoke.

"How could you tell it was Marjorie?" Sarah asked.

"Who else would it be?" Mom said.

It was true. "She's being a space alien," Sarah explained.

"Well," Mom said, "as long as she's having a good time."

"It's for a movie. For her video production class." Sarah watched as the little boy nodded at everything Marjorie said. "I was supposed to be the alien."

"What happened?"

"Chorus rehearsals."

They watched in silence.

"Hmm," Mom said. "Maybe she'll direct another movie and let you be in it. Maybe something with better costumes." She paused. "A Civil War drama, maybe."

"I don't think so," Sarah said.

Mom turned around. "Really?" She peered at Sarah intently. "Have you two had a fight?"

"Not exactly."

"What's up?"

Sarah didn't want to tell her. Mom would only say that she had made a promise to Marjorie that she hadn't kept, that she never kept her promises, that it was just like saying she would dust her room.

"Nothing. Everything's fine." She opened the door and got out of the car. "Just tell me if she calls."

She slammed the door harder than she meant to, but she could still hear Mom inside the car saying, "Just go talk to her."

No way, Sarah thought. No way am I talking to her.

But she found herself walking out to the soccer field anyway. It was too weird to pretend Marjorie wasn't there.

The closer she got, the more she could hear.

"We should leave tape space between the scenes," Marjorie was saying.

"Should I turn the camera off?" the little boy asked.

"No, just fade in and out. And use the pause button. It looks unprofessional to have a blank screen," Marjorie said. Her glasses had slid halfway down her nose. Sarah knew she would have pushed them up if her hands weren't stuck inside her costume. "You'll see when we get to the editing room."

Then she noticed Sarah and stopped talking.

"Hi," Sarah said.

"Hi."

They just stood there. It was weird, feeling so awkward. Sarah couldn't think of anything to say. The little boy watched them.

Finally Sarah said, "The costume looks great."

"Yeah," Marjorie said. "It's a good thing you're only a little bit shorter than I am. Louellen just had to fix the hem."

"It looks great," Sarah said. "Really great."

She knew she sounded like an idiot. But it was as though her head were full of mud and the gears in her brain just wouldn't turn.

"Are you Sarah?" the little boy asked.

"Oh, sorry," Marjorie said. "Joey, this is Sarah Franklin. Sarah, this is Joey Hooper."

Sarah was shocked. Joey came up to her shoulder. His voice was still high, and his hair was cut in a bowl shape with bangs, like a little kid's. Most seventh grade boys had shaggy hair or buzzcuts.

"Hi," Joey said. "Sorry you couldn't be in the movie."

"Me, too," she said.

Sarah looked at Marjorie, who was hopping around, trying to bend forward to push at her glasses with her arm, and didn't seem to hear what was being said.

"It would have been better with all three of us," Joey said. "This way we can only have one character in the shot at a time."

"I'm really sorry," Sarah said. "I already told Marjorie I was really sorry."

Marjorie didn't say anything.

"And it would be nice," Sarah said, surprised to hear the beginning of yelling in her voice, "if she could say it was okay."

Marjorie looked up. "I *did* say it was okay," she said.

"And mean it!" Sarah shouted. "Not just say it and act like you're being all forgiving, when really, you're mad."

"I'm not mad! Don't say I'm mad! You don't know how I feel!" Marjorie yelled back. Her eyestalks were bobbing like crazy. "I *said* it was okay!"

It scared Sarah that Marjorie was yelling. She had never heard Marjorie yell before. It felt as though if they didn't stop yelling, they were going to teleport themselves to a different universe, like on the old *Star Trek* shows Marjorie loved. A universe with red oceans and blue trees and inhabitants who read minds and didn't need air to breathe. A universe where they weren't friends anymore.

"I'm *always* saying it's okay!" Marjorie yelled.

The words reverberated in the air around them as Sarah realized that she'd been wrong all those times when she'd thought Marjorie didn't get it.

Marjorie had gotten it all along.

Joey watched them with his mouth hanging open.

"It's not my fault!" Sarah thumped her fists against the sides of her thighs in frustration. "I can't get out of chorus! Do you want me to just forget about rehearsals? Do you want me to flunk?"

"No." Marjorie's glasses were a little fogged up, but Sarah could see that behind them, she closed her eyes.

"Well, what do you want me to do?"

"Nothing." Her eyes were still closed. "Nothing."

"I don't know how to make it right!" Sarah said.

Without meaning to, she had made it into a question.

"You guys are like my sisters," Joey said. "Except they hit each other."

"Just forget about it," Marjorie said. "Can't you just forget about it?"

Marjorie wouldn't forgive her. Sarah knew she wanted to stay angry and hurt a little longer. Maybe to hold it over Sarah's head. Maybe just to feel superior. It seemed unfair to Sarah that she wouldn't just let it go, when Sarah kept saying she was sorry, over and over.

"Lizzie gets that it's not my fault," Sarah said. "Why can't you?"

Marjorie opened her eyes. They stared at each other for no more than a few seconds, but to Sarah it seemed like hours: protracted, interminable. Marjorie's eyes were hard and blue, not giving anything away, like the eyes on a marble statue.

"We have to get back to work," she said. "It might rain. We have to get going."

Behind her, Sarah heard the distant sound of voices singing scales, and knew that she was already late.

"Marjorie—"

But Marjorie turned her back. She hopped toward Joey and craned her neck to see into the camera's viewfinder. Sarah knew she was being shut out, that it was Marjorie's way of pretending she wasn't there.

It was like being erased.

"Fine," Sarah said. "Fine! Be a baby! Who cares? Not me!" She turned and began to run back to the auditorium. "Not about you or your stupid movie!" she yelled over her shoulder.

Marjorie didn't yell anything back, but Sarah knew she had heard every word. The silence behind her was louder than yelling.

On Monday, Sarah found Lizzie and Carly between periods.

"Marjorie isn't going to hang out with us anymore," Sarah said.

"Thank God!" Carly said. "No offense, but she was really getting on my nerves."

"What happened?" Lizzie asked.

"It's too complicated to explain." Sarah was afraid

that if she tried, she might cry. "I'm sick of even think-ing about it."

"You can eat with us," Lizzie said.

"Thanks."

"It was bad, her eating with us," Carly said. "I could tell people were wondering what *she* was doing with *us*."

"That's really mean," Lizzie said.

"Well, I don't care," Carly said. "I'm sorry, but I don't. You know it's true. We're different from her. The way we dress, how we talk. What we talk *about*." She pulled her jean jacket closed and folded her hands under her crossed arms to keep them warm. "People should be friends with people who are like them."

Out of habit, Sarah wanted to defend Marjorie, but she stopped herself. She didn't have to anymore.

Also, some of what Carly said was true. They *were* different from Marjorie. They talked about hairstyles and boys and clothes. Marjorie talked about old movies. They wore cool sneakers and jeans and hoodies. Mar-jorie wore clogs and overalls.

"It's too hard to be friends with people who are too different," Carly said.

"You shouldn't say that stuff," Lizzie said ner-vously.

"Why not? It's true," Carly said. "I'm sick of pretending to like everyone. I like people who wear cute clothes and eat normal things for lunch."

The bell rang.

"Marjorie is gross," Carly said.

"Shut up!" Sarah said, shocked at herself, at how angry she was. She never said "shut up."

Carly looked at her with wide-open eyes.

"She is not gross!" Sarah yelled. She could feel tears in her eyes and at the back of her throat.

"Don't tell me to shut up!" Carly said.

Kids were pushing past them, trying to get to class. But Sarah was frozen in the middle of the hallway. She felt that if she moved, it would be like telling Carly to think whatever she wanted about Marjorie.

Even if she and Marjorie weren't friends anymore, she couldn't let Carly say she was gross.

Lizzie pushed between them and grabbed each of them by the elbow.

"Come on, you guys," she said, moving them forward in the hall. "Carly, quit being so heinous."

"I'm not being—"

"Just shut up, then," Lizzie said, letting go of Carly and steering Sarah into a deserted bathroom. She closed the door, and Sarah burst into tears.

Once she started, Sarah couldn't stop, not even when the bell rang, letting them know that third period had started.

"You're going to be late for PE," she burbled to Lizzie, who was standing by silently, handing her paper towels for her runny nose.

"It's okay," Lizzie said. "It's too cold for calisthenics."

"But you'll get in trouble. Your mom will be mad."

"My mom's always mad."

It was embarrassing to cry in front of someone else. The tears felt inexhaustible, like rain pouring from a cloud in Sarah's head that wouldn't empty.

Lizzie didn't say anything. She just kept handing over paper towels.

Snot poured out of Sarah's nose. She started to hiccup.

"This is disgusting," she said, wiping her face with another towel, willing herself to stop sobbing.

Lizzie shrugged. "I cried like that when my dad left. And when my dog died," she said. "Sometimes life is just really sad. And you have to get it out of you."

Sarah nodded and hiccupped. "I'll be all right. Just go to class," she said. "Please. It's okay. I'll be all right," she said again.

"Are you sure?" Lizzie peered at her as though she

were a vase that had fallen and shattered, a dangerous mess of sharp, broken parts.

"I'm sure."

Lizzie gave herself a quick glance in the mirror, then looked back at Sarah. "It's for the best, maybe," she said softly.

Sarah felt the back of her throat ache with new tears. She forced herself to swallow them. "I just have to sit here a minute," she said. "To let my face go back to normal."

Lizzie nodded. "Don't be too late," she said. "Mrs. Fogelson makes you do extra homework problems if you're too late."

When Sarah was sure Lizzie had disappeared down the hall, she cried a little longer. She told herself it was to get rid of as many tears as she could so they didn't start leaking out in the middle of doing complex fractions.

But really it was because she was so angry. That Carly was hateful, and also a little bit right. That Marjorie wouldn't just try to be like everyone else, even if it was only in public, for a few hours a day. That everything changed, whether you wanted it to or not. That nothing was fair.

CHAPTER 10

THAT NIGHT, Grandpa arrived unexpectedly at five.

"Dad, I didn't know you were coming, or I would have made more for dinner," Mom said.

"Not here to eat," he said. "I'm here to take ole Henry to the park."

On hearing his name, Henry, who had followed Mom and Sarah to the front door, stood tall. His tail wagged madly.

"We're going to practice heeling, aren't we, boy?" Grandpa said.

"Can't you teach him some tricks?" Sarah asked. "Heeling is just walking. He already knows how to do that."

"We're going to teach him how to do it right," Grandpa said. "Want to come along?"

Sarah was cranky and hungry. "No, thanks," she said. Then she added, "It would be more fun if it was tricks."

Grandpa bent low, fastening Henry's leash.

"I'm thinking of entering him in the All Good Dogs Day contest this summer," he said.

All Good Dogs Day was held in July. There was a dog parade, a dog talent show, an obedience competition, and awards for Best Dog Costumes. You could buy regular ice cream and doggy ice cream. Grandpa had tasted the doggy ice cream once. He said he was glad he wasn't a dog.

"He's already a good dog," Sarah said. "I don't see why he has to win something to prove it."

"He doesn't have to. But I think he's got the competitive spirit. He likes learning new things. I think he'd like a trophy with his name on it. An award or something."

"It's too bad there's not an award for face-peeing," Sarah said. "He'd win that."

Henry was eyeing Grandpa intently. Sarah realized he was waiting for Grandpa to hold a treat overhead, the signal that he was supposed to sit.

"We should be careful about feeding him too many treats," she said. "Henry might get fat."

"Don't worry," Grandpa said. "I'm getting him into fighting shape."

He said it as though Henry were a boxer in training for an important bout. Sarah looked at Henry—his hopeful, alert eyes—and wondered if he would care about beating other dogs. She wished everything didn't have to be about winning, but somehow, that's how it always ended up.

Henry had lowered himself to the ground, but not close enough to Grandpa's feet. "No treat until you do it right," Grandpa said.

She was a little mad at him, which she almost never was, for taking something that had been just for fun and making it into something that had to be worked at and practiced and done just right.

For the next two weeks Mr. Roche made them sing every day after school and for five hours on Saturdays and Sundays. Sarah felt as though all she did was sing and eat and do homework and sleep. She could feel herself beginning to hate singing. Her throat hurt. Sometimes she wished Handel had never been born.

But then a funny thing happened. She could hear herself singing better. She sounded in tune all the time.

She could hold the notes without having to take another breath. She could sing her part even when the sopranos were singing theirs.

"Come on, altos!" Mr. Roche boomed, his arms thrashing out the beat. "Stick with it! Come on!"

Lizzie and Sarah exchanged looks, then concentrated on his baton. Sarah could feel her breath in her abdomen, right where it was supposed to be. She sang, and the words of "The Lone Wild Bird" stopped being just words. Her lungs were full of music. Her heart grew large with sound and feeling.

"Not bad," Mr. Roche said. He wiped the sweat off his forehead as he riffled through the pages of his score. "Not bad."

He wouldn't look at them, but Sarah knew he was proud.

At lunch on the Tuesday before the competition, she asked Lizzie, "Have you noticed that you hear those songs in your head all the time?"

Lizzie rolled her eyes. "I *dream* about them," she said. "I wake up, and it's like I've been listening to 'Praise the King' in my sleep."

"You know when we're all singing together and in tune and it's just, I don't know, *right?* And then we stop, and it's like the air around us is vibrating?" Sarah brushed chocolate chip cookie crumbs off her lap.

"Sometimes, just walking around, I feel like that. Like the air is buzzing from all the music in my head."

"You guys are bizarre," Carly said. "It's just singing."

Sarah and Carly hadn't mentioned Marjorie since their fight two weeks before, but they hadn't made up, either. Mostly they just talked about boys and pretended that the fight never happened. But Sarah noticed that Carly seemed a little less welcoming of her, a little more willing to be unreservedly critical.

"It's like there's music everywhere, and the only way you can hear it is by singing so much," Sarah said.

Carly licked mustard off the tip of her thumb. "I'm going to try out for tennis," she said. "My mom says tennis is a good sport to do because you can do it when you're grown up. And also, you get to wear cute little skirts."

"Tennis makes me too sweaty," Lizzie said. "I can't do sports that make you sweat. I sweat enough just from having so much hair."

"You guys should do a sport," Carly said. "Sports are cool. Unless it's something like bowling."

"I don't like sports," Sarah said. "Playing or watching."

In PE, she didn't like caring so much about winning; it made her feel as though she were being chased. Even when the teachers said that winning didn't matter, that what counted was teamwork and good sportsman-ship, they still liked it when you won.

Sarah's dad and Diane watched sports on TV all the time. When baseball was over, they switched to foot-ball. After football season ended, they watched basket-ball. Sometimes, if they got desperate, they even watched golf. Sarah got the feeling that they watched sports because it kept them from thinking too much about things that were hard to think about. That if they turned off the TV, they'd have nothing to say to each other.

"Who has time for sports, with all this singing?" Lizzie said.

"You guys should be careful," Carly said. "Singing is kind of weird."

Sarah felt everything freeze, the way it did between the time when you burned yourself on the hot iron and the moment when you screamed.

"What," Lizzie said, turning to Carly, "are you even *talking* about?"

"Everyone knows that cool people do sports and weird people do music," Carly said. When she saw Lizzie's mouth drop open, she added, "But it's okay. Singing is much cooler than *band*. Band people are really weird. I mean, *tubas?* What kind of a normal per-son plays the *tuba?*"

"What about the flute?" Lizzie asked sarcastically. "Can you be normal and play the flute?"

Carly considered this seriously.

"I guess so," she said. "If you're doing it to get into college or because your parents are making you."

"So you mean," Sarah said, "it's normal to play the flute if you don't want to, and weird if you do?"

"Hey, I'm not making this up," Carly said. "It's common knowledge. Ask anybody. Music people are weird."

"That is the stupidest thing I've ever heard," Sarah said. "If it's common knowledge, how come Lizzie and I never heard it?"

"Look, it doesn't matter," Carly said. "I like you even if you're weird. It's not like I'm not going to be your friend or anything. I'm just telling you. I'm just trying to *help*. So you can get into a sport before it's too late."

"When is it too late?" Lizzie asked. Sarah could tell by her eyes that she felt as though Carly were jabbing her with a fork.

"By next year, everyone already knows how to play everything," Carly said. "So when you try out, you never get picked. You have to start a sport by seventh grade or it's hopeless."

Even though Sarah didn't like sports so far, she thought it was possible that she might like them someday. She didn't want to think that she couldn't change her mind about sports in high school, that there was a deadline that the people in charge had neglected to mention.

"How do you know all this?" she asked suspiciously.

"Everyone knows," Carly said.

"*I* didn't," Lizzie said.

"It's because you're singing all the time," Carly said. "If you're not hanging out with cool people, you miss a lot of information."

The night before their trip to L.A. they had Cotillion. Sarah and Lizzie got to the gym early. Lizzie looked glum.

"I can't stop thinking about what Carly said," she admitted as they stood by the back wall watching everyone else surge toward the refreshment table. "Do you think we're weird?" she added, her voice a whisper.

"No," Sarah said. She watched a few boys stuff some cookies into the pockets of their suit jackets. You were only supposed to take two. "Well, not weirder than anyone else. I mean, everyone is a little weird. Don't you think?"

Lizzie shook her head. "Not Alison Mulvaney. Not Steve Birgantee."

"Maybe they are," Sarah said. The mom at the refreshment table was holding out her hand, waiting for the boys to give back the cookies. "Maybe Alison secretly listens to fifties music. Maybe Steve is afraid of the dark and sleeps with a night-light. Things that, if *we* did them, would be weird. But because they do them, they're not."

"I don't understand why Alison and Steve get to decide what's cool," Lizzie grumbled. "They run the school, and no one else gets a say."

Gloomily they watched the crowd.

"I don't think Carly's my best friend anymore," Lizzie said.

Sarah could tell she was about to cry. "I'm sorry," she said.

"I can't stand what she said about singing being weird," Lizzie said. "If she doesn't get it about the singing . . ."

"I know," Sarah said.

"Don't say anything when she gets here," Lizzie said. "Just pretend everything's okay. I don't want to have a big conversation about everything here."

Sarah nodded, but she had stopped paying attention. Marjorie had entered the gym. She was wearing another crazy old dress. This one had puffy sleeves and a bustle. She wasn't wearing a hat this time; her hair was in a bun, held in place by a black knit snood. Kids were staring and pointing at her, but she was pretending not to notice. She looked out over the crowd, as though she was waiting for someone.

"At least we have each other," Lizzie said.

Sarah smiled. It was nice to feel that she and Lizzie were getting closer, that they both knew what it felt like to lose a best friend, that by being sad about the same thing together, they were getting to know each other better. But then she caught sight of Marjorie and felt the happiness drain out of her like bath water. She and Lizzie had each other, but Marjorie had no one. The thought made Sarah's heart feel as though someone were stepping on it.

Lizzie had turned her attention back to the boys.

"Jason Webb is wearing orange socks!" she said, craning her neck to see. "Can you believe it?"

Sarah was about to look when she saw Joey Hooper, hair slicked back, wearing a suit that was way too big for him, making his way toward Marjorie.

It had never occurred to her that Marjorie actually was waiting for someone.

"And black sneakers instead of hard shoes!" Lizzie said. "He is so disgusting."

Joey and Marjorie began talking immediately. Marjorie had to bend forward because Joey was so short. Joey pulled a crumpled piece of paper out of his pants pocket and handed it to Marjorie, who read it and began to laugh. Sarah wondered if Joey had been working on the script for their movie, if they'd decided to add some jokes.

Or maybe they had jokes of their own that had nothing to do with the movie. Just jokes that best friends had.

"His pants should be longer," Lizzie said. "If his pants were longer, you wouldn't be able to see his socks."

Sarah nodded, barely hearing a word Lizzie said.

Grandpa was at the house when she got back. He was training Henry to sit and stay.

"Another thing he already knows how to do," Sarah said.

"How was Cotillion?" Grandpa asked, following her into her room, where Mom had started to pack. Henry trotted along behind them, eyes still fixed on Grandpa's pocket, bulging with treats.

"Okay," Sarah said. "We did the fox trot."

"Ooh, the fox trot!" Mom stood at the dresser, refolding shirts that Sarah had stuffed into the drawers. "I wish I'd learned all that stuff when I was your age."

"Why didn't you?" Sarah asked.

"We didn't foxtrot much in those days," Mom said. "We did a lot of disco."

"We do that in a few weeks," Sarah said.

Mom had gotten out the black vinyl suitcase that was almost never used. She set a stack of Sarah's shirts into it.

"Now, your grandfather," she said. "Ask *him* about foxtrotting."

"Really, Grandpa? You can foxtrot?"

Grandpa lowered himself to the bed. Henry leaped up beside him, turned himself awkwardly around, and sat hard against Grandpa's hip.

"In my day, I was quite the hoofer," Grandpa said.

"Do you know what a hoofer is?" Mom asked.

"Like Gene Kelly," Sarah said.

Mom turned around to stare at her. "How do you know who *he* is?" she asked.

"I just do." She pulled her hoodie over her head and began to fold it. "Did you dance with Grandma?" she asked Grandpa.

"Grandma didn't like to dance much. She said all that bouncing around embarrassed her," Grandpa said. "So I said, 'Lucille, I'd rather dance *with* you, but if I can't, then I'm dancing *without* you.' She grumbled a bit, but she didn't mind. 'As long as it gets you out of the house,' she said."

Mom and Sarah smiled. They could just hear Grandma.

"So I joined a club," Grandpa said. "We danced for fun, mostly. Sometimes we competed."

"Did you win anything?" she asked.

"A few trophies."

Sarah loved when Grandpa talked about his past. Most of the time he told her something she had never known about him before. It made her feel as though she was always getting to know him better, and also, as though she had barely begun to know him at all. There was always more to find out.

It was reassuring to think that life could be so full of experiences that you could recount them for years and always have more to add. Maybe, Sarah thought, you could accumulate enough happy memories so that the bad ones dimmed and receded and ultimately disappeared altogether.

"I gave it up when I stopped drinking," Grandpa said, his gnarled, knuckled hand playing in the scruff of Henry's neck. "I still kinda miss it."

Mom was staring into the suitcase, hands on her hips, counting sweaters.

"Show her," she said to Grandpa, not turning away from the suitcase.

"Naw." Grandpa shook his head. "Sarah doesn't want to dance with an old codger like me."

"Yes, I do," she said. "Come on, Grandpa. I even have the right music."

She opened her desk drawer and pulled out one of the CDs Mr. Roche had burned for them.

"Frank Sinatra?" Grandpa said, looking at the cover. "What are you doing with Frank Sinatra?"

"My choir teacher says to listen to his phrasing," she said, putting the CD in the player.

"Well, I'll be damned," Grandpa said.

She pulled on one of his arms.

"Come on, Grandpa," she said again.

He hesitated, then slowly eased himself off the bed. It was hard to do, with his fake leg.

"Take it easy, Dad," Mom said. She bent down and began picking up clothes and old homework assignments off the floor. "I don't want you tripping on all this junk."

Sarah ignored her and held out her arms as "The Best Is Yet to Come" filled the room.

"Mrs. Gretch says to hold my elbow like this," she said.

Grandpa took her hands in his.

"Forget about Mrs. Gretch," he said. "Just follow me."

They danced for half an hour to "The Best Is Yet to Come" and "It Happened in Monterey," "Look at Me Now," and "Young at Heart." Sarah could have kept going, but finally Grandpa had to stop. "Damn leg," he grumbled, settling himself back on the bed next to Henry and Mom, who had given up on folding clothes and watched, smiling, as the dancers rocked and turned in the small, cluttered room.

"I forgot how good you were," she said, putting her hand on Grandpa's arm. "But be careful, Dad. Don't overtire yourself."

Grandpa rubbed his thigh. "That was fun," he said, a little out of breath.

"It's so much better dancing with you than with Dylan Dewitt," Sarah said. "I didn't even have to watch my feet. I just felt the music."

"Now you're getting it," Grandpa said.

"Yes, you are," Mom said. "You looked very graceful, very confident."

"I didn't even know what I was doing," Sarah said. "But then I stopped thinking. I stopped trying. And then I was just doing it."

"That's the idea," Grandpa said. "Your body does the right thing when your brain gets out of the way."

They all laughed, even Mom, who Sarah could see was still worrying about Grandpa's leg.

"You should try it, Mom," she said.

"I don't want Grandpa to strain himself," Mom said, but she looked wistful, as though she had been left out of something magical.

Sarah held out her arms. "I'm not tired at all," she said. "But you have to promise that you'll never tell anyone that I danced with my mom."

Mom pushed herself off the bed and stood squarely in front of Sarah. Sarah took her hands and met her gaze head-on.

"I promise," Mom said solemnly.

They danced to "The Lady Is a Tramp" and "New York, New York" and "Let's Fly Away," until Mom insisted they stop, that they had packing to finish. Energized despite all the exercise, Sarah acquiesced, even though she didn't want to stop. She could have danced for hours. It was so much fun to do something without worrying about whether it was cool, about what other people would have said if they had seen her.

CHAPTER 11

ON WEDNESDAY MORNING Sarah found the choir kids assembled in the front parking lot, watching as their bags were loaded into the school bus that would take them to the airport. She had said good-bye to Mom in the car, assuring her that she would call every night she was gone, that she wouldn't go to any public bathrooms alone, that she would follow directions and not get lost. It was a relief to shut the door and put a definitive end to her mother's lectures and warnings.

Mr. Roche stood at the open bus door, frazzled and short-tempered, running his hand through his hair and checking and rechecking his clipboard.

"Are we all here?" he yelled. "Where's Molly? Where's Jason? How many times did I tell you, people? Be on time!"

"It's kind of stupid that he's telling *us* that," Lizzie said to Sarah. "We're the ones who *are* on time."

"We better not miss that plane," Sarah said. She liked being early for things, for once not minding Mr. Roche's franticness.

Mr. Roche began calling the names of kids who hadn't yet turned in their medical information forms.

"You better have it now," he said. "No one gets on the plane without one."

"I heard Jason Webb has a glandular condition," Lizzie said.

"Really?" In truth, Sarah wasn't that interested. She was bored. Even a field trip with plane rides and hotel rooms involved a lot of just standing around.

"When we flew to Hawaii, it took almost six hours," Lizzie said. "Flying to Los Angeles takes less than an hour. They don't even have time to serve you food."

"Just peanuts and a soda," Robert Whitchurch said, sidling up to them, a green duffle bag slung over his shoulder. "We go to Disneyland twice a year. Not because of me. Because my parents are weird."

Lizzie glanced quickly at Sarah, trying to telegraph her excitement on Sarah's behalf. Sarah knew Lizzie was trying to be discreet, but she cringed inside, certain that Robert could see everything that passed between them.

"What's weird about your parents?" she asked.

Robert shoved his hands deep into his pockets. He was tall and thin, with tousled, wavy black hair, shockingly white skin, and a small mole near the corner of his mouth. Sarah felt herself resisting the urge to brush the mole with her fingers, as though it were a crumb that needed dislodging.

"They love Disneyland. They went all the time before I was born," he said. "Actually, they go less now, because it's more expensive with three of us."

"You're lucky," Lizzie said. "When we go on vacation, my mom makes me go to museums. And also to visit old relatives."

"I'm pretty sick of Disneyland," Robert said. "I want to go camping."

"We did that once. Before my parents got divorced," Sarah said, remembering. "We rented a camper because my mom said it wasn't a vacation if she had to sleep on the ground and cook in the dirt. We drove to the Grand Canyon. I remember how the desert was full of flowers. And that the Grand Canyon looked like the inside of a steak cooked medium rare."

Robert laughed. "Cool."

"The best part was the mule trip around the rim of the canyon," Sarah said. "My mule's name was Smoky. He had the softest ears."

"I always mix up mules and donkeys," Lizzie said.

She was standing with one hip jutting out and was twirling a strand of her long, curly hair around one finger, something Sarah had never seen her do before.

"Mules are a cross between donkeys and horses," Robert said. "Donkeys are just donkeys." He laughed again. "I always know completely useless information that no one else really cares about."

Lizzie laughed loudly. To Sarah, she sounded a little like a donkey.

"Me, too!" Lizzie said. "Like, I know exactly how high the Empire State Building is. Twelve hundred fifty feet. And also when the bikini was invented. Nineteen forty-six."

Robert, Sarah noticed, kept sneaking glances at her, even as he nodded along with Lizzie and said, "I usually know mostly science stuff." She tried to feel happy that he seemed to want her to join in the conversation, but she didn't, momentarily overcome with a wave of sadness. The truth was that the best part of the Grand Canyon trip hadn't been Smoky's stiff, velvety ears. The best part was that her parents had laughed and told jokes as they sat in the camper's front seats, remembering trips they had taken years before she was born, trying to agree on which state they'd been in when the policeman had pulled them over for speeding, pointing out roadside trees and flowers that struck them as beautiful or strange. Sarah had sat in the camper's broad back seat, lulled by her parents' pleasure, enjoying the unfamiliar sensation of feeling relaxed in their presence.

Even then, in some mysterious way, she had known that it wouldn't last.

It wasn't the fact of her parents' divorce that made her sad now. It was something subtler, harder to pin down. The more she thought about it, the more she realized that she grieved because she didn't want to tell Lizzie or Robert about how it had really been, sitting there in the back seat, listening to her parents' recollections of happy times, catching glimpses of flowers as red as lips, as startling as a phone call from someone you never expected to hear from again.

"On the bus!" Mr. Roche called, stuffing his clipboard under his arm and cupping his hands around his mouth. "Choir kids! Here we go!"

In the ensuing pandemonium Sarah noted that Robert wandered awkwardly toward a group of boys, embarrassed by the possibility of having to sit on the bus with a girl. Lizzie grabbed her arm.

"We have to sit next to each other," she said. "If I get stuck next to Jason Webb, I'll be sick."

Sarah and Lizzie sat next to each other on the plane as well. Sarah grabbed the window seat, promising that

Lizzie could have it on the trip home. Lizzie settled herself in the middle seat and seemed happy enough until a large older lady with a helmet-like bouffant took the aisle seat and positioned her left arm on the armrest. "Heinous," Lizzie whispered, turning her head just slightly in Sarah's direction. She looked at the magazine Sarah had grabbed from the seatback in front of her. "What are you reading?"

"'Emergency Procedures,'" Sarah said. Having never flown before, she wasn't nervous exactly, but the flight attendant's listless pointing toward the doors seemed alarmingly insufficient.

"I never read that stuff," Lizzie said. "Planes never crash."

"I know," Sarah said, thinking but forcing herself not to say, You can't be too careful.

On takeoff, the plane's engines thrummed under her seat, and the plane itself began its roll down the runway, quickly gathering momentum. Just when Sarah thought that her chest would explode from the roar and speed, everything tipped delicately upward. Beneath her, the world she had always known began to look small and different and far away.

"There's the Bay Bridge," Lizzie said, pointing.

Sarah watched as the city's spires, gray and sparkling under a cloudless fall sky, disappeared behind her. Now they crossed the bay, then the crowded freeway. The cars looked like beads strung tightly on a thin bracelet.

"That's where my cousins live," Lizzie said, pointing to impossibly small houses cluttering a hillside.

Sarah couldn't take her eyes off the ground below, even after Lizzie, a veteran of plane trips to Hawaii, New York, and Miami, had pulled a fashion magazine from her carry-on bag and begun to study pictures of holiday shoes. The world was different from what she had thought: smaller, grayer, more crowded. Or maybe it wasn't. Maybe it just depended on where you were when you looked at it.

She said so to Lizzie after the flight attendant had set plastic cups of ginger ale on their tray tables. Below, rolling hills, still gold and gray, as yet untouched by green, looked like a row of soft puppies asleep against their mother.

"I guess," Lizzie said.

"But doesn't it make you think?" Sarah asked, unwilling to be disappointed by Lizzie's lack of interest. "From up here, nothing seems important. From down there, everything does."

"Everything's important up here," Lizzie said. "Nothing's different." She craned her neck, searching for the flight attendant, ignoring the old lady who held her book with one outstretched arm, peering through thick glasses and moving her lips as she read. "Where are the peanuts? Robert said they give you peanuts."

"Something's different," Sarah said. But maybe it wasn't the world. Maybe she herself was different, unrecognizable to herself without her parents or her grandpa to talk to, her town's streets to walk down, her teachers to question, her TV shows to watch. She felt as though the world she had left behind was a person waving a cheerful goodbye and also signaling to her from below, trying to get her to pay attention, trying to tell her something. But she kept that to herself, knowing Lizzie didn't really care, that it would have sounded weird.

The flight attendant brought them peanuts, but before they could finish them, the plane dipped down and the FASTEN SEAT BELT sign flashed on. "Not enough time to get bored!" Lizzie said, stuffing her magazine back in her bag. Sarah nodded agreement, even though she hadn't been bored at all. For the first time in a long time, she could hear herself think. Her own voice inside her head had been long unheard, not foreign, exactly, but only distantly remembered.

She was sorry when the wheels touched the earth, once again ordinary, and the plane skidded to a stop.

The Southland Motel was the kind of place Sarah's mom wouldn't have liked, a place where she would have checked the sheets before she paid, to make sure that they'd been changed. Lizzie and Sarah got a room with twin beds, a wooden table, and a TV screwed into the wall.

"There's no ice machine," Lizzie whined, flopping onto one of the beds. "And the pool is disgusting."

"It's too cold to swim, anyway," Sarah said, sitting gingerly on the other bed. The blue and green spread was thin and discolored.

"Where's everybody else?" Lizzie asked just as they both heard a knock.

Opening the door, Sarah saw Robert Whitchurch, Jason Webb, and Sean Souza standing awkwardly in the outside hall.

"We're next door," Robert said. "We've only got two beds, though. One of us has to sleep on the floor."

"It's not gonna be me!" Jason said. He laughed loudly, as though he'd made a joke.

From her bed, Lizzie eyed him disdainfully.

Sean Souza was wire-thin, with shaggy hair that nearly eclipsed his large, dark-lashed eyes. Lizzie had long been of the opinion that his passionate interest in fencing, which required the wearing of tights, interfered with his cuteness. "We'll take turns," he said. "That's only fair."

"I have scoliosis," Jason said. "My parents will sue the school if I don't get a bed."

"Shut up," Sean said. "There's nothing wrong with you."

"It's *mild* scoliosis!" Jason yelled.

Robert looked apologetically at Sarah. "You're lucky," he said, just to her. "These guys keep fighting."

"Maybe Mr. Roche can get you into a different room," she said.

Robert smiled. "It's okay. I kind of like seeing what it's like to live with other kids." He tipped his head to the side and raised his shoulder, as though he were trying to insert it into his ear. Sarah realized that she had seen him do this before. Maybe, she thought, when he was nervous.

"It's too bad about not having enough beds," she said.

"I brought a sleeping bag, just in case," Robert whispered. "I'm not telling them that, though."

When he smiled, his eyes actually twinkled, like in a Saturday morning cartoon.

"Smart," she said, smiling back, wondering if her eyes twinkled, too, but doubting it.

Lizzie had risen from the bed and now stood behind her, arguing with the boys.

"Oh, come on!" she yelled at Sean. "I've seen pictures!"

"They're not tights!" Sean yelled back. "They're nylon pants!"

"That's just as bad!" Lizzie said.

"Fencers don't wear tights! My father wears tights when he cycles in cold weather, so I know," Sean said.

"Your dad wears tights?" Jason asked, bursting into laughter.

"Nylon pants are exactly the same as tights, in terms of heinousness," Lizzie said. She turned to Jason. "And you should shut up. At least Sean does something cool with swords. You are just disgusting."

"How do you know I don't do something cool?" Jason asked. "Something I don't have to wear tights to do?"

"Well, do you?" Lizzie sounded to Sarah as though she was pretending not to be interested.

"I play poker," Jason said. "I'm the best poker player in my family."

"I'll bet," Lizzie said, but less derisively than Sarah would have expected.

Mr. Roche emerged from a room across the parking lot. He carried his clipboard and a briefcase, which Sarah knew contained his favorite baton and all his scores.

"Keith School Choir! Outside, please!" he called from the middle of the parking lot. "The bus is leaving NOW!"

"How embarrassing," Lizzie whispered.

"Nobody even cares," Jason said. "We're the only people in this dump anyway."

Lizzie gave him a sour look, probably, Sarah surmised, out of habit. But Lizzie didn't argue with him; she just gathered her purse and her music folder from the bed and followed the boys out into the hall, letting Sarah lock the room behind them.

The bus didn't leave for another twenty minutes, during which Mr. Roche lectured from the aisle next to the driver about respecting authority, listening to directions, staying focused, and remembering that they were representatives of their school. As he droned on, Sarah watched the motel maids wheeling their carts full of cleaning supplies from room to room. They parked the cart outside when they entered each room to make the beds and vacuum the carpets. She tried to think of one nice thing about working as a maid and couldn't. Maybe people who worked as maids just liked for everything to be really clean, she thought. Maybe it made them happy to leave a room with sparkling sinks and crisp sheets still warm from the dryer.

Even as she thought it, she knew it probably wasn't true, that the maids hated this job, or were just doing it for the money and didn't think much about it one way or the other. But it made her feel better to imagine a nicer story, one in which the maids woke up excited to go to work, happy and fulfilled to be scrubbing tooth-paste off of mirrors and pulling hair out of shower drains. Maybe, Sarah thought, at home at night, they even told their children stories about the funny things people left behind on nightstands and under the beds.

"Wherever you go, whatever you do," Mr. Roche said, "remember that you are being watched. Be proud, be polite. Be a credit to yourself."

A fairy tale, she knew. But she couldn't help it. The truth—the way things really were—was sometimes almost too much to bear.

CHAPTER 12

THE CALIFORNIA MIDDLE SCHOOL
Excellence in Music Competition was being held at a local
community college. The bus deposited them in front of a
building that housed the music department. Mr. Roche
showed them rooms acoustically designed for band and
orchestra rehearsals, classrooms where students sat facing blackboards scrawled with musical notation as fragile
and ornate and unreadable as ancient hieroglyphics.

"Maybe some of you will major in music someday,"
he said.

Sarah raised her hand. "Can you major in music if
you want to do something else for a living?" she asked.

"Certainly," he said. When he noticed Sarah's expression, he added, "You don't have to decide anything
right this minute."

She knew he was joking, but she couldn't help trying to picture how her parents might react if she told them that she was majoring in music and then planning to be a physical therapist anyway. Her mother would still wonder why she wasn't going to be a doctor. Her father would think that she should focus on just one thing. Diane would probably take her aside and whisper something about trying to join a sorority.

She hated admitting that Mr. Roche's not-so-subtle effort to inspire them had worked, but she noticed that when they finally began their practice session in a room reserved specially for them, they sounded better than they had in their own school music room. Her voice sounded clear in her ears, and strong, as though it could stand alone and also, paradoxically, as though it was one small part of a greater, more complicated whole. The music, she realized, needed every voice to be what it was meant to be, to be perfect. It bloomed around them like a gauzy tropical flower, each of their voices a root that nourished it.

"Let's try it again," Mr. Roche said.

For once, it didn't feel like nagging. They sang it again, and it was even better the second time, and better yet the third.

* * *

They sang for two hours. As the afternoon sun began to cast long shadows on the walls, Mr. Roche ran both hands through his hair. "Enough," he said. "We don't want to overtire ourselves."

"Like this is tiring for *him*," Lizzie said, stretching her hands over her head.

"I feel as though I've been exercising for two hours," Sarah said. "Like I've been doing nonstop sit-ups."

"Hey, Mr. Roche, can we get pizza?" Jason shouted over the din.

Sarah thought Mr. Roche might object or say something to Jason about raising his hand. But he only nodded.

"Excellent idea," he said.

The pizza place was down the street from the college, the only store on the block that was not devoted to computers and electronics. A harried-looking waitress asked Mr. Roche, "How many in your party?" and when Mr. Roche said, "Twenty-three," she rolled her eyes. "I gotta split you up," she said.

They commandeered three tables. Mr. Roche and the two chaperones—Mrs. Worth and Mr. Souza—sat at one. Sarah noticed happily that Robert seemed to be watching her surreptitiously, waiting for her to take a seat before he committed himself. When she and Lizzie sat down, he grabbed a chair opposite them. Beneath the table, Lizzie pinched her knee. Sarah forced herself not to flinch, for fear of making Lizzie's excitement even more obvious.

"Nothing with olives," Jason said, sliding into the chair next to Robert. "I'm allergic to olives."

"Let's get sausage," Sean said, taking the chair on the other side of Robert. "Sausage is the best."

"Pepperoni's better," Jason said.

"You're an idiot," Sean said.

Robert looked up from his menu and caught Sarah's eye. She smiled, knowing exactly what he meant.

"Quit it, you guys," she said. "We can get more than one pizza."

Lizzie was eyeing Jason with her usual contempt. "You better not get any pepperoni stuck in your beard," she said. "I might throw up if you do."

"It's not a beard," Jason said. "It's a goatee."

"It's disgusting," Lizzie said. "Nobody else our age has one."

"What can I say?" Jason was flushed with what looked to Sarah to be a combination of embarrassment and pride. "I'm highly developed. I'm advanced."

"You're an advanced idiot," Sean said.

"Look who's talking," Lizzie said.

Robert set his menu down and leaned toward Sarah to be heard.

"I can't eat sausage or pepperoni. I'm a vegetarian," he said.

"Wow." She had never known a vegetarian before. "Is it because of your crazy parents?"

"No. They think *I'm* crazy." Robert shrugged his shoulder toward one ear. "My mom says if she'd known how hard it was going to be to feed me, she'd have given me back to the doctor and asked for a different kid. She's kidding, but she really hates the way I eat."

"Why do you do it?" Sarah asked.

"I don't know," he said in a way that made Sarah know that he did.

"It doesn't seem very fair to the animals," she said. "But I really like meat. I don't think I could give it up. Is it hard?"

"In the beginning. But you get used to it."

"I don't know if I could," she said.

She searched his face, trying to see if he looked disappointed. As far as she could tell, he didn't. She was relieved. She didn't want to think that Robert might like her for something that wasn't really a part of who she was.

"Do you like mushrooms?" Robert asked tentatively.

She nodded, happy to be able to give a truthful answer that he would appreciate.

"And onions," she said. "And olives, actually."

"You want to split one?" he asked. Leaning even closer and tilting his head slightly in Jason's direction, he said, "It would be fun to torture him with the olives."

She laughed. It occurred to her for the first time that she liked Robert, really liked him, that his dark hair and twinkly eyes were just an added bonus, that he could be a friend.

As the waitress set their pizzas and sodas before them, Sarah realized that she was starving. She hadn't eaten anything except for the peanuts on the plane since breakfast.

"Olives!" Jason said, seeing what they had ordered. "Gross!"

"Shut up!" Lizzie said, but she watched with interest as he took a paper napkin from the chrome dispenser and gently patted the top of his pepperoni-dotted slice. "What are you doing?" she asked.

"Getting rid of the extra grease," he said. "Cheese is greasy."

Lizzie didn't answer, but Sarah noticed that she, too, blotted the top of her slice with a napkin, and Sarah wondered if Jason's fastidiousness might outweigh the heinousness of his goatee in Lizzie's eyes.

They ate their first bites of pizza in relative silence. Everyone, Sarah realized, was hungry. At other tables, patrons looked to be college students: Sarah didn't see many families. The absence of children made her feel like an adult, as though she had stumbled through a time-space portal and happened on a universe peopled solely by teenagers. Only Mr. Roche and the chaperones were older. Sitting primly at their table, sharing a pitcher of beer, they seemed grossly out of place and maybe even a little nervous, as though they might be asked to leave if they called attention to themselves.

"It must be weird having your dad as a chaperone," she said to Sean.

"Not really," Sean said. "He knows he's supposed to ignore me."

"If my mother was a chaperone, she would have made me sit with her," Lizzie said. "She would have made me sleep in the same room."

"I'm the youngest of five kids. My dad's been chaperoning a long time," Sean said. "He knows about not talking to me and not trying to make a big deal out of being my dad."

"He probably wouldn't let us stay up all night and play poker," Jason said.

"You guys can't stay up all night," Lizzie said. "The competition's tomorrow. Mr. Roche said we have to be asleep by ten."

"Will you shut up?" Sean whispered. "Will you stop telling everybody our business?"

"I'm telling Mr. Roche," Lizzie said.

Sarah nudged Lizzie's thigh with her knee. "Don't," she said.

"Why?" Lizzie fixed Sarah with an incredulous stare. "Don't you want to sound good? Don't you want to win?"

"Well, yes," she said. "But I still don't think you should tell."

Sarah didn't quite know how to say what she felt: that telling Mr. Roche would be a betrayal, that the boys probably wouldn't sing as well if they couldn't play poker, even if it was only out of spite. That keeping their secret would enhance their bond as friends, and that alone would make their singing stronger.

Lizzie turned to the boys. "If you let us play, we won't say anything," she said.

"Do you even know *how* to play?" Sean asked.

"Not really," Sarah said.

"I can play mahjong," Lizzie said. "And hearts."

"Great," Jason said. "I don't even know what mahjong *is*."

"It's Chinese," Lizzie said. "You play with little tiles. With these really cute drawings on them."

"Well, you play poker with *cards*," Jason said. "And plastic chips for betting."

"Ooh," Lizzie said. "Chips."

"I only know how to play gin," Sarah said sadly. Betting sounded like fun.

"We'll teach you," Robert said.

"Oh, come *on*, man," Jason groaned. "It's too hard to teach people. It takes too long."

"No, it doesn't," Robert said.

Sarah heard something authoritative in his voice, something the boys heard, too, because his pronouncement seemed to settle the matter.

"Do you even know about the hands?" Jason asked Lizzie.

"What hands?" Lizzie asked.

Jason sighed heavily. "The order? One pair, two pair, three of a kind?"

"Not exactly."

Jason clasped both hands to the sides of his head in outsize despair.

Sean laughed. "This is going to be great," he said. "They don't even know how to play!"

"What's great about that?" Jason moaned.

"Girls? Betting?" Sean raised his eyebrows in a knowing way.

"What about girls and betting?" Sarah asked.

"Girls are stupid about betting," Sean said. "They always bet too much."

She felt resentment rise up in her throat.

"They like playing with the chips," Sean said. He held a pretend chip between his thumb and index finger. "I bet a hundred dollars," he said, affecting a girly voice.

"You're an idiot," Lizzie said.

"A total idiot," Sarah said, which was unlike her: she didn't usually call people names. But it bugged her the way he was talking about all girls. She could tell that he wasn't really talking about betting, that he was used to making generalizations about girls, that he'd heard his father and brothers do it, that he didn't even bother to think about the truth of what he said or whether he might hurt people's feelings.

"We're not going to bet a *lot*," Robert said.

"It's okay," Sarah said, a little irritated by his nervousness, his need to make everything all right for her. "In fact, I bet we win," she said, looking directly at Sean, who squirmed under her gaze and grabbed another piece of pizza, then tried to stuff it into his mouth all at once.

She recognized the gesture as one of false bravado; for a moment she felt powerful and sure. Lizzie held up her hand for a high-five. But as Sarah finished the last of her slice, she wondered if what Sean said was true. Did girls bet too much?

There was a ring of truth to it, something in her own experience that seemed to confirm her doubt.

CHAPTER 13

AT TEN O'CLOCK Sarah and Lizzie were in bed when they heard the expected knock on the door. In the dark, Sarah leaped from her bed and unlatched the door.

"Everything all right?" Mrs. Worth asked.

"Everything's fine," Sarah whispered. When Mrs. Worth tried to peer over her shoulder into the darkened room, she added, "Lizzie's already asleep."

"Oh," Mrs. Worth whispered back, nodding her head, as though she was pleased to be allowed in on an elaborate joke. "If you need anything, just call my cell."

"We'll be fine," Sarah whispered. "But thanks."

"Sleep well!" Mrs. Worth said, tiptoeing off to check on another room.

Sarah closed the door. Lizzie sat bolt upright and

threw off the covers. She was still dressed in the jeans and sweatshirt she had worn to rehearsal.

"Shhh!" Sarah cautioned from the door. "Wait until she goes back to her room!"

"You get dressed," Lizzie said. "Where are my shoes?"

They flipped on the bedside lamp and Sarah fumbled for her clothes. When she was dressed, Lizzie knocked on the wall adjoining the boys' room. Someone knocked back.

"We could get sent home for this, you know," Sarah whispered, but the thumping in her chest was causing pleasurable fear rather than terror. It was thrilling to break rules for once, to take a chance.

"Oh, it's just curfew," Lizzie said. "It's not so bad."

"But Mr. Roche said—"

"Quit worrying!" Lizzie examined herself in a hand-held makeup mirror. "You want some lip-gloss?"

"No, thanks." Sarah took a deep breath, willing herself to relax. "Maybe we should tell them we'll only stay an hour."

Lizzie pursed her lips together to even out the gloss. She snapped her mirror shut.

"Let's not make any rash decisions," she said. "Let's just see how it goes."

Sarah liked for things to be planned. She liked to

know what was coming. But she said "Okay" and thought that if nothing else, she would get the opportunity to show Sean Souza what a moron he was.

They sat in a circle on one of the beds. Jason, wearing a tinted green plastic-billed visor, shuffled the cards.

"Okay, the two players to the left of the dealer are the 'blinds,'" he said. "That's you guys," he added, looking at Sean and Robert. "Sean, you're the little blind, and Robert, you're the big blind. So Sean, you put in one chip, and Robert, you put in two. Just to make sure that there's something in the pot."

Robert and Sean each surrendered their chips. "A chip is worth a penny," Robert explained to Sarah and Lizzie. Sarah couldn't help but notice that he looked just at her when he said it, though.

"Now, I'm going to deal everybody two cards, but you have to leave them face-down. You can look at them," Jason said seriously, as though he were a doctor explaining to a patient how he was going to take out the appendix. "They're called the hole cards."

"Why?" Sarah asked.

Jason sighed. "I don't know. It doesn't make any difference. That's just what they're *called*," he said.

"Why are you wearing that heinous hat?" Lizzie asked.

"It's not a hat. It's a dealer visor," Jason said. "It's what all the dealers in Las Vegas wear."

"My grandma wears a hat like that when she plays golf," Lizzie said.

"Can we just *play?*" Sean said.

"It's all right," Jason said. "She can ask questions."

"Not fashion questions," Sean said. "Questions about the game."

"Okay," Jason said. "Now we have to bet. Sarah, you start, since you're to the left of the blinds."

"How do we know how much to bet?" Sarah asked.

"Everybody started out with a hundred chips. That's a dollar," Robert said. "Just bet a little bit to start."

She tossed two blue chips into the center of the bed. They clicked against each other in a crisply satisfying way.

"Do I have to bet the same amount Sarah did?" Lizzie asked.

"You can if you want. Or you can raise her bet. That means you add more," Jason explained. "Betting is really complicated. My dad bets on horseraces. He hedges bets, which is kind of like betting on both sides. It's a way to make sure you don't lose too much. A way to protect yourself."

His earnestness made him seem smarter than he usually did in chorus, Sarah thought. He didn't seem like the same kid who was always losing his place in the music and coming in a full measure ahead of where he was supposed to.

"If you don't want to bet anything, you can fold," he went on. "The only thing you can't do is bet less than Sarah."

"Hmm." Lizzie bit her lip and squinted.

"Oh, come *on!*" Sean said. "Just do it already!"

"Quit yelling at her," Jason said. "Quit acting like you're such a big expert."

Lizzie smiled at him, then pulled two chips from her pile and placed them carefully into the pot.

"Now you've seen her two. That's what you say," Jason explained.

"Thanks," Lizzie said. She beamed as though she had mastered something complicated.

When they had all placed their bets, Jason discarded the top card on the deck.

"That's called burning. So if people saw the top card, they can't cheat," he said. He turned the next three cards on the deck face-up in front of him. "They're called 'the flop,'" he said.

"Whose cards are those?" Lizzie asked.

"They're community cards. Eventually there will be five cards in the community pile," Jason explained.

"You have to figure out how to use those five cards plus the two in front of you to come up with the best hand."

"This is really confusing," Lizzie said, but she smiled at Jason, as though she meant to imply that he was really smart for understanding such confounding rules.

Sarah was confused, too, but she didn't say so. She knew that Sean would purposely confuse befuddlement for stupidity, and she didn't feel like having to defend herself against his taunts.

They all bet again. Robert, she noticed, had organized his chips in small, neat stacks of five, which he took pains to preserve on the wrinkled, sloping surface of the bed. She liked that he was orderly; she imagined his room at home—clothes folded and put away, pens and pencils nestled in the drawers of an immaculate desk.

Jason burned another card, then turned the next one face-up on the community pile.

"That's the 'turn,' or 'Fourth Street,'" he said.

"I love how everything has cute names," Lizzie said.

They bet again. Sarah had a pair of jacks. She raised Robert's bet by a chip and shot Sean a dirty look.

"The fifth card is the 'river,' or 'Fifth Street,'" Jason said. He pushed his visor back off his forehead. "That's it. Now we bet for the last time and show what we have."

"Can you go over the hands again, please?" Lizzie asked.

"Sure," Jason said, ignoring Sean's exasperated sigh. "High card, one pair, two pair, three of a kind. A straight is five cards in order, but not in the same suit. A flush is five cards in the same suit, but not in order. Full house is three of a kind combined with a pair. Then comes four of a kind. Then a straight flush: five cards in order in the same suit. And then a royal flush, which is ace, king, queen, jack, and ten in the same suit."

"That's what you've got, I bet," Sean said, smirking at Sarah.

She ignored him. The last community card, a two of clubs, had given her another pair. Two pair, she realized, wondering if she might have won.

"How do you remember them all?" Lizzie asked. She was gazing at Jason with newfound admiration and sounded a little breathless.

"Practice," Jason said. He reddened a little but looked happy about Lizzie's question. "You'll remember them once you get used to playing."

"Now what do we do?" Sarah asked, eager to win, to shut Sean up.

Jason turned his gaze from Lizzie and said to the

group, "The player who made the last raise shows his hand first. Let's see. That's you," he said, nodding at Robert. "Whaddya got?"

Robert turned over his cards. Two pair, just like Sarah, only one of his was a pair of queens. She felt her heart turn over in disappointment. She had really wanted to win.

She consoled herself with the fact that she beat Sean, who had a pair of sixes, and Lizzie, whose highest card was a ten of diamonds.

Jason gathered all the cards and expertly began to shuffle. "So everybody's clear? Everybody gets it?" he asked.

"Sort of," Lizzie said. "I might still need some help."

"I get it," Sarah said. "Just deal."

She ignored Sean's snort of mirthless laughter—clearly his effort to pretend that her two pair beating out his sixes had been a weird, unrepeatable fluke—and Lizzie's wide-eyed stare. She hardly recognized herself: usually she was the girl who didn't care about winning, who shrugged it off when her teammates in PE teased her for not being able to sink one basket, who played Parcheesi with Grandpa only if he promised to take her out for ice cream after.

Winning, despite its stress and anxiety, despite the possibility of *not* winning, was pleasurable.

It was as though she had discovered a new, previously unimagined part of herself. As though her nose or her hair had been irrevocably altered, and looking in a mirror, she didn't recognize the face that looked back.

They played until one in the morning, until Jason finally said, "We'd better stop, you guys. We have to meet the bus at eight o'clock." He barely stifled a yawn.

"No fair!" Sean cried.

Sarah gazed at the meager puddle of chips in front of him.

"Yeah," she said, smiling. "No fair that you're the biggest loser."

When he blushed deeply, she was suddenly ashamed of herself. Winning, she decided, was infinitely more fun than rubbing it in.

"Sorry," she said quickly.

Unmoved, Sean said, "I could beat you any day. You just had beginner's luck."

"Pretty good luck," Robert said. "She came in second."

"Yep. Second," she said, letting her hands play in the chips she had won. Too many to stack. "And it wasn't luck."

The game over—and, with it, the necessity of pretending that any sort of comeback was possible—Sean pinched one of his chips between two fingers and held it over his head, a phantom basketball. He flicked his wrist in the effortless way of athletic boys, then watched as the chip arced through the air and clattered into the metal wastebasket under the desk. *"Yes!"* he hissed, holding both fists aloft in triumph.

"It wasn't luck," she said again, knowing he was just faking bravado, but wanting him to hear her all the same.

Half an hour later, snug beneath the scratchy motel sheets, she was almost asleep when Lizzie asked, "Do you think Jason is sort of cute?"

Sarah smiled in the darkness. "Not really," she said. "That beard."

"I don't, either," Lizzie said quickly. "But it's not really a beard. It's a goatee, he said."

"It's still gross," Sarah said.

"It's not really even a goatee," Lizzie said. "It's more like stubble in just a few places."

They were silent for a moment.

"Isn't it amazing how good he is at poker?" Lizzie asked.

"It is kind of surprising," Sarah said. "He doesn't make you think he'd be good at anything."

"I liked how he just knew all the rules. How he explained everything so clearly." She was silent again. "That was really fun," she added.

"Really fun," Sarah said, nodding for emphasis, even though she knew Lizzie couldn't see. "Maybe we can play again tomorrow night."

"Tomorrow's the party with all the other schools. After the competition."

"Oh," Sarah said, disappointed. She had forgotten.

"I think maybe Jason's a little cute," Lizzie said.

They were quiet again.

"Do you miss Carly?" Sarah asked, whispering in case Lizzie had fallen asleep.

"Sometimes," Lizzie answered groggily. "Just when I remember certain things. Or when I want to tell her something."

Sarah stared up into the darkness, which was like an empty black bowl turned upside down, a mini night sky, starless and thick.

"Me, too," she said, wondering if Lizzie knew that she wasn't talking about Carly anymore.

CHAPTER 14

THE CHOIR KIDS staggered into the South-land Motel's breakfast area at seven thirty the next morning. The girls wore the white button-down blouses and knee-length black skirts required for concerts; the boys wore white dress shirts and black slacks. The rules about attire were strict. Mr. Roche made Jason take out his father's cuff links.

"They're for good luck!" Jason said.

Mr. Roche shook his head. "They're against the rules," he said.

"Why?" Jason whined.

"Jason. Please." Despite his usual franticness, Mr. Roche seemed weary. There were bags under his eyes, and the tuxedo he was wearing looked shapeless, as though anxiety had caused him to lose weight. "Not today."

Jason looked as though he was about to argue, but at the last minute he said only, "Okay."

"Have a bagel. Have a doughnut." Mr. Roche raised his voice to include everyone. "Eat up, people. Breakfast is important. You want to be at your best."

Sarah and Lizzie staked out two chairs near the coffee urn. Sarah pulled the shell off a hard-boiled egg, feeling obliged to eat something even though she wasn't hungry. Lizzie fished for individual cereal squares in a miniature box of Cinnamon Chex. She popped each square into her mouth and then licked the pads of her fingers for extra cinnamon.

Sarah was glad that Lizzie wasn't in the mood for talking. She herself felt talked out. It was hard to share a room with someone, she realized, hard to answer someone else's questions and make polite small talk while brushing your teeth. Maybe it wasn't so hard for kids who had brothers and sisters. But she was used to being an only child. It was lonely sometimes, but nice not to have to talk when you didn't feel like it.

Everyone else was less raucous this morning than they had been yesterday. Perhaps the excitement of the flight and the motel check-in and dinner in a new restaurant had given way to sleep deprivation: the beds at the Southland Motel were lumpy and unfamiliar, and cars traveled the nearby freeway all through the night. Or maybe it was the imminence of the competition itself, casting a pall, forcing seriousness. She wasn't sure, but as she chewed her egg, Sarah relished the chance to sit quietly, to let talk and noise wash over her without responding.

She turned her attention to the only people in the room who were not part of their group—an elderly couple in matching khaki pants, blue Windbreakers, and enormous white sneakers. The lady had an old face that didn't match her dyed brown hair, which was pulled into a sloppy topknot. She wore silver wire-rimmed glasses and walked with a stoop. Her husband wore a battered fishing hat studded with pins from well-known tourist destinations. Without appearing to stare conspicuously, Sarah could make out one from Hearst's Castle, another from the Carlsbad Caverns. His hands were speckled with age spots and shook slightly as he poured nondairy creamer into his Styrofoam cup of coffee. Sarah guessed that they were driving a motor home around the country, that they had lots of grandchildren who waited avidly for their postcards, that they listened to radio ministers as they drove through all the national parks. She wondered if they argued, or if they had run out of things to say to each other. She wondered what it was like to know someone so well for so long. If you just got tired of each other, or if the mere fact of all those years of intimate acquaintance made you love each other more.

Edna and Frank, she decided. Frank was a retired high school principal who liked to fish. Edna was a housewife who became a librarian for a while after her kids grew up, but she got sick of it and quit. She'd had enough of telling noisy kids to be quiet.

Sarah's daydream was interrupted by Mr. Roche, who stood at the doorway, clipboard under one arm.

"Keith School Choir!" he called, as though the old couple might otherwise think that his announcement was meant to include them. "Let's get going, people. The bus is waiting!"

Edna smiled as everyone crumpled cups, rummaged through backpacks, tossed crumb-littered napkins into the wastebasket under the doughnut tray. She seemed to enjoy the bustle and din. Maybe not a librarian, Sarah decided. Maybe an attendance secretary who made kids sign out when they had dentist appointments in the middle of the day.

Sarah had a hard time thinking of jobs that didn't have to do with schools.

She hadn't realized that she was staring at Edna until the old lady smiled directly at her. "You're a member of a chorus?" she asked. "You sing?"

"Yes," Sarah said, remembering, or maybe just

knowing without ever having been told, to say yes instead of yeah to an older person.

"How nice," Edna said. She nudged Frank and said very loudly, "Did you hear that, dear? They sing."

Frank winced and put his hand to his ear. Sarah saw that he wore a hearing aid.

"Quit yelling!" he grumbled. With a shaky hand he brought his coffee to his lips and took a noisy slurp.

Edna leaned behind him, her hand on his back, and mouthed, "He's a little deaf," at Sarah. Then, in a normal tone of voice, she said, "What do you sing?"

"'Sing for Joy' by Handel. 'Shenandoah.' 'The Lone Wild Bird,'" Sarah said.

Frank tried to shrug Edna's hand off of his back.

"I heard you!" he said, sounding angry and agitated. "This damn coffee's too hot!"

"Ooh, Handel! I love Handel," Edna said, her hand still resting gently against Frank's back. "Aren't you lucky to be a singer!"

"I'm not really a singer," Sarah said, noticing that Mr. Roche was waiting impatiently at the door, trying to hurry everyone out to the parking lot. "It's just a class."

"Well, of course you're a singer," Edna said. "I wish I could sing. But I have a tin ear."

"I said I heard you!" Frank said.

"My second grade teacher told me I sang in the key of H," Edna said.

"I'm sorry. I have to go," Sarah said, beginning to back away. From her grandfather, she knew how old people liked to keep talking, even when you made it clear that you didn't have enough time.

"Bye!" Edna said. She raised her hand from Frank's back and waved merrily. "Sing your heart out!"

As the bus pulled into the busy street, Mr. Roche reminded them yet again about staying with the group, behaving in a dignified way, not laughing or talking out of turn, listening to the judges who were assigned to critique their performance. Sarah had heard it all before.

She couldn't stop thinking about Frank and Edna, how cranky he was, how sweetly Edna touched his back, even when he tried to shrug her away, even when he seemed to bristle at the idea of needing her. How did she do it? Sarah wondered. How did she tolerate his deafness, his crabby dismissals, his coffee-stained pants, the result of those shaky, hairy-knuckled hands? Did she just love him so much that none of those things mattered?

"Dignified, people!" Mr. Roche bellowed. "No giggling. No shoving in line. No peculiar noises emanating from mouths or other orifices!"

All the boys laughed.

"Heinous," Lizzie whispered.

The mood in the bus shifted dramatically as the bus pulled into the college parking lot. Without being asked, everyone stopped talking. Sarah saw Robert fiddle with the buttons of his shirt cuffs. Sean Souza, who had been slouched down low in his seat, long legs in the aisle, suddenly sat up straight.

"Cell phones off," Mr. Roche said. "Let's go."

They followed him into the Music Building, whose main foyer was full of middle school kids in formal attire. All the boys wore white shirts and dark pants, but the girls' clothes were different. Girls from one school wore matching floor-length navy blue dresses with high necks and puffy sleeves. Girls from another wore black turtlenecks and black slacks.

"I like the dresses best," Lizzie whispered. "Why can't Keith School get those?"

"They're probably too expensive," Sarah whispered back.

"I hope we don't get judged on what we wear," Lizzie said.

"We're really good," Sarah said. "That should be enough."

She wanted to win. But it was a different feeling

from wanting to win at poker, a game she didn't really care about and barely knew how to play. Last night, she realized with surprise, hadn't really been about wanting to win. She had wanted to beat Sean.

But now, falling in line with the others behind Mr. Roche, who was running his fingers around the back of his neck, making sure that the collar of his tuxedo jacket was lying flat, she heard her own voice in her head saying calmly, Please let us win.

It wasn't a prayer. She wasn't asking. She was urging herself to do the best she could.

They stood in a semicircle on the dimly lit stage, the judges well hidden in the auditorium's shadowy darkness. Facing them, Mr. Roche tapped his baton on the music stand and raised his arms. Uncharacteristically, he met their eyes and winked. It was his way of telling them they had worked hard, that he was proud.

Sarah felt the curious sensation of her body tightening and relaxing at the same time. She opened her mouth, her lungs ready to fill with air, the music at attention inside her, waiting to be released.

They sang for twenty minutes, but when they had taken a bow and begun to file offstage, it seemed to her as though they hadn't even started. She wished they had prepared more songs. She could have sung for hours.

They found out that they won two hours later, after the last chorus had sung, after the judges had deliberated and announced the results on the stage of the now-packed auditorium. Sarah jumped to her feet with her choir mates and whooped for joy. She threw her arms around Lizzie.

"We did it!" Lizzie whispered in her ear, and Sarah hugged her harder, amazed at how proud she was, how good it felt.

And puzzled, too, because she had thought she wouldn't care so much.

On the bus back to the motel, Mr. Roche stood in the aisle. He looked naked without his clipboard, which he'd left on his seat.

"Attention, people!" he called, his feet wide apart to brace himself against the stops and starts. "We're invited to a party tonight."

The boys began to chant, "Par-ty, par-ty," and dance in their seats. Sarah laughed; these were the same boys who shuffled awkwardly around the dance floor at Cotillion, who shoved whole cookies into their mouths and forgot to wipe the crumbs off their lips.

"It's for all the choirs who took part in the competition." Mr. Roche had to yell to be heard. "And even though it's a party, we're still going to be on our best behavior. Is that clear?"

"It's a good thing I brought my Cotillion stuff," Lizzie said to Sarah. "What are you going to wear?"

"Just jeans." Would everyone else have thought to bring fancy clothes? Sarah began to worry. What if she was the only one in jeans and a hoodie? And then, suddenly, the worry disappeared, evaporated like a pool of water on hot cement.

So what if she was the only one?

"Is there going to be dancing?" Molly Worth called out.

"There's going to be music, but no dancing," Mr. Roche said. "You apes can't dance."

Everyone laughed. A few boys hooted and scratched themselves under their armpits.

"Maybe I'll wear jeans, too," Lizzie said.

The party was held in the foyer of the Music Building at the college. The room was crowded with the same kids who'd been there earlier in the day. Everyone wore jeans.

To the left of the front entrance, a table had been set with platters of deviled eggs, cheese and crackers, sliced ham and turkey, rye bread and sourdough rolls, and chocolate chip cookies. Women in black pants and stiff white shirts filled cups with soda and bottled water.

"You know how at Cotillion the moms make this

big deal about eating neatly and not spilling? And how by the end of the night, the boys' shirts are stained and crumby?" Sarah said to Lizzie. "Isn't it funny how no one's spilling anything here?"

"I think it's the fact that they have to wear suits," Lizzie said. "I think they can't move right. Or maybe the suits are too tight and cut off circulation to their brains." She took a careful bite of deviled egg and surveyed the room. "See any cute boys?"

"Not really," Sarah said, pretending to look. Really, she was just trying to spot Robert.

"Are we supposed to be talking to all these kids we don't know?" Lizzie asked. "I hate that."

"We can talk to anyone we want," Sarah said. "It looks as though everyone is just hanging out with people they already know."

"Then what's the point of having a party?"

Sarah folded a piece of ham onto a roll and took a bite. "Let's just go up to some people we don't know and say 'hi,'" she said.

Lizzie stared at her. "Really?"

"Well, what *is* the point of having a party? You just said."

"But what if no one says 'hi' back? Or what if they say 'hi,' and then no one can think of anything else to say?" Lizzie looked as though Sarah had just suggested that they make a running leap from one ten-story rooftop to another.

"Oh, come on." Sarah felt bad at the impatience in her voice. "We'll think of something," she added, forcing herself to sound encouraging. "Let's just do it."

"But what if—?"

"Come on," she said again, putting her hand firmly on Lizzie's back, propelling her forward. "Be brave."

Standing near the door to the auditorium was a cluster of kids. They were all munching on sandwiches and cookies, concentrating on tidy eating, momentarily not talking. Sarah recognized one of the girls from earlier in the day.

"Were you wearing those cool long dresses this morning?" she asked, gently inserting herself into their circle.

The girl she recognized had nearly black hair and blue bangs so long that they hung over her black-framed glasses like a patio awning.

"Yeah," she said, smiling. "I dyed my hair to match."

"Cool. I'm Sarah, by the way. And this is Lizzie," she said, stepping to the side, allowing Lizzie in.

"Oh, we loved your dresses," Lizzie said. "Those were the coolest uniforms here."

"I'm Daisy. And this is Jeanette and Paul and Lindsay." Daisy gestured feebly at her friends. "Where are you from?"

"Keith School, near San Francisco," Lizzie said.

"Ooh, you guys won!" Jeanette beamed with excitement. She was the kind of girl, Sarah knew, who pretended that everything was exciting. "That is so amazing!"

"Thanks," Sarah said.

"You guys always win," Paul said. "We suck."

"We pretty much suck, too," Lizzie said. Sarah knew she was saying it just to be nice.

"We suck more, though," Paul said. "If there was a contest for sucking, we'd win."

They made conversation for a while. Sarah learned that they were from Deer Mountain Middle School in Fresno, that their choir director had hair plugs but pretended he didn't, and that the best thing about Deer Mountain was one of the science teachers, who let you listen to your iPod while you did experiments.

They talked until more kids from Deer Mountain joined the group and eventually overtook the conversation. Sarah thought that maybe she and Daisy might exchange e-mail addresses, but in the end, that seemed pointless, a gesture that would have felt insincere. "See ya," she said, and Daisy smiled warmly and said, "Yeah, okay." It was just right.

"They were nice," Lizzie said as they inched their way back to the food table. "It was good that you made us go talk to them."

"It's not so bad talking to new people," Sarah said. "I used to hate it." She remembered the first time she and Lizzie had gone to the Juice Warehouse after school: how hard it had been to think of things to say, how important it had seemed to fill in all the pauses with more words.

"You're good at being friendly," Lizzie said.

"You're friendly, too," Sarah said, flushing at the compliment.

"Yeah, but I'm only friendly if someone else has been friendly first," Lizzie said. "It's hard for me to be first."

Sarah tried to remember back to the first days of chorus. Hadn't Lizzie made the first overtures?

"People like you," Lizzie said. "People feel safe with you."

"Really?"

Lizzie nodded. "Everybody," she said.

"Not everybody," Sarah said. "Alison Mulvaney said I was a loser."

They had reached the snack table, where the crowd had thinned considerably after the last chocolate chip cookie had been eaten. Still, Sarah lowered her voice when she said it. She felt ashamed, as though she had committed a gross faux pas in public.

Lizzie laughed and shook her head. "Remember that first time we went out for smoothies?" she asked.

Sarah nodded.

"The next day, Alison cornered me in the hallway. She asked me why we were at the Juice Warehouse. Like, were we working on a class project together? Or did we each go separately and just happen to run into each other? I said no, that we'd gone together, that we were friends."

"Why was she asking?" Sarah said. "Why did she even care?"

"When I said we were friends, she said I should be careful, that you never liked anyone but Marjorie. That she tried to get you into her group and you weren't interested."

"What group? With Zannie and Yvonne?"

"That's what she said." Lizzie pulled her hair off her neck and puffed upward, trying to cool herself with her own breath. "It's hot in here!"

"They never wanted me in their group," Sarah said. "But I wouldn't have wanted to be in it anyway. And not because of Marjorie. Because they're mean."

"Well, that's what she said," Lizzie said. She fanned the back of her neck with her hand. "I didn't tell you, because I knew it was stupid."

"Of course it's stupid," Sarah said, but less vehemently, with less certainty, thinking it was funny that Alison would have told Lizzie such a lie when she had called her a loser in the girls' bathroom.

"I mean, it's not like there's some rule that you can only have one friend," Lizzie said.

CHAPTER 15

THE NEXT MORNING on the flight back, Sarah sat next to Robert. She had been intending to sit next to Lizzie, but during preboarding, Lizzie had begun asking Jason Webb about the details of various poker games and had become so engrossed in his answers that she and Robert had agreed to switch seats.

Now, as the plane soared above the gray, barren land below, Robert said, "My parents won't believe we won. They'll want to see a trophy or a plaque."

"My dad will say if I like winning so much, I should try out for soccer or baseball. He won't get it at all," Sarah said.

Just saying it made her sad.

"My mom will be proud, though. And my grandpa," she added.

"Have you ever heard of Knights in the Round?" Robert asked. Without waiting for an answer, he went on. "It's a men's a cappella group. They sing madrigals and rounds. Without instruments," he added, as though she might not know what "a cappella" meant. "My parents got me two tickets for my birthday. They said I could bring a friend."

"Cool," she said, trying to breathe through the bubbly chaos that had suddenly erupted in her body. Realizing that she knew what was coming, that it was what she thought she had wanted all along.

Robert hunched one shoulder toward his ear, then said softly, "You want to go with me?"

She breathed and smiled. She thought, Lizzie will kill me.

"I can't go on dates with boys until high school," she lied. "My mom's pretty strict about that."

Maybe it wasn't a lie. Now that she thought about it, she imagined that her mom had rules about boys and dating. Rules that hadn't yet been articulated, but existed nonetheless.

All she knew was that she wasn't ready. Dating hinted at new obstacles, new complications for which she still felt unprepared. She was just starting to get the hang of friendships. Friendships were hard enough.

"Oh," Robert said. His eyes, cast downward, refused to meet hers. She was surprised to see how crushed he was. She had forgotten to think how hard it had been for him to ask.

"Is the show sold out?" she asked.

He barely shrugged.

"Because if there are more tickets, maybe we can try to get more kids to go. I could go if there was a group," Sarah said. "Lizzie and Jason, maybe."

Robert brightened a little. "I'll ask my mom. She bought the tickets," he said. "That might be fun."

He sounded, to Sarah, a little relieved.

"Yeah," she said, turning to watch as the cars and houses—ant-size, unreal—slowly came into clearer view beneath her. Enlarging, they became the things they really were, hinting more concretely at the people who drove and lived in them, their pleasures and sorrows and wonders and aches, their complicated lives.

"Maybe we can all get together for poker night once a week," Robert was saying.

"Sure," she said as the plane touched down and her own life came rushing up to meet her.

Mom made a special dinner—meat loaf with strips of bacon on top, mashed potatoes with garlic and sour cream, a salad, and brownies for dessert—to mark her return. Grandpa arrived, even though Friday was usually the night he had dinner with his Alcoholics Anonymous friends. "Missed you," he said, hugging Sarah against his side.

"I was hardly gone at all," she said, glad anyway for the hug.

"Seems like more time than it was," he said.

At the table, she told them about the plane rides and the motel, the rehearsals, the competition itself. How exciting it was to win.

"Of course it was!" Grandpa said.

"I thought the *singing* would be fun. But winning—"

"Winning just means other people thought you did a good job," Grandpa said.

"It always feels like it's about beating someone. If you win, then someone else has to lose."

"Well, whoever it is you beat will win the next time. Or the time after that," Mom said. "Everyone knows a little of both, eventually."

Sarah considered this. It struck her as extraordinarily comforting.

"You want to help me train Henry for the All Good Dogs competition?" Grandpa asked. "Get him ready to beat the pants off those damn German shepherds?"

"What's wrong with German shepherds?" Mom asked.

"They think they're so smart," Grandpa said.

Mom and Sarah laughed.

"Yeah," Sarah said. "Yeah. That sounds like fun."

Henry, stationed beside Grandpa's chair, cocked his head at her. He seemed proud of himself, ready for whatever would come next. She pulled a corner off her strip of bacon, saving it for him for later.

She told them about playing poker.

"Hah! Texas Hold'em! Haven't played in years!" Grandpa pushed his chair away from the table to give his middle more room. "Did you win?"

"I came in second," Sarah said.

"I don't want you betting," Mom said.

"Oh, relax!" Grandpa said. "It's part of the fun. You gotta bet. You gotta know what's at stake."

"I don't want her getting in over her head," Mom said.

"It was just a few cents," Sarah said, but she knew that her mother wouldn't be appeased, that there was something in the very nature of betting that made her anxious and apprehensive.

"Second's not bad, for the first time," Grandpa said, giving Sarah a sly wink.

"Don't encourage her, Dad," Mom said.

"Mom, it's okay," Sarah said, but tenderly, feeling protective of her, understanding that her caution was just her way of showing love, and also that it was warranted, that the world was full of real danger and heartbreak.

"She just needs to be smart. Keep her cards close," Grandpa said, which Sarah thought sounded like real wisdom, the truest thing she'd ever heard.

Tuesday, at Cotillion, she noticed that everyone was dancing better. No one stepped on her feet. No one's hands were slimy with sweat. It was easier to relax in a strange boy's arms, to tell herself that making a mistake wasn't so terrible, that it was just dancing.

She danced the polka with Dylan Dewitt, who was thrilled to take advantage of what he deemed permission to leap around the room.

"It's not even dancing!" he yelled happily over the accordion music, thundering forward, not appearing to notice whether Sarah could follow him or not. "It's like pole-vaulting or something!"

"It's supposed to be dancing!" she yelled back crabbily. "That's why there's music!"

Immediately he slowed his pace.

"Sorry," he said, breathing heavily. "I guess I got carried away."

"It's okay," she said, relieved to hear that the song was coming to an end. Across the room, she saw Robert trying to catch her eye, signaling that he would make sure they were partners for the fox trot.

Over Dylan's shoulder, she caught sight of Marjorie and Joey Hooper. Marjorie wore a floor-length black skirt and a starched white blouse. The top of Joey's head came only to Marjorie's collarbone, but he held her firmly in his arms. Their steps were careful, almost sedate. They looked as though they were trying to polka with dignity, something Sarah realized was almost impossible to do. She thought of Edna and Frank at the Southland Motel: the way Edna overlooked Frank's surliness, the way she explained everything that people said. The way she was patient. Sarah wondered if Joey Hooper even noticed the oddities and quirks that were so much a part of Marjorie. She hoped that he was patient with her.

"Thanks for the dance," she said to Dylan when the music ended. It was what Mrs. Gretch had told them to say, but she meant it. Jumping around the room hadn't felt like dancing, but it was fun.

"No problem," Dylan said, forgetting that "You're welcome" was the proper response. His huge front teeth gleamed under the fluorescent gym lights.

Behind him, Joey Hooper put one hand before him and one hand behind and bowed from the waist. Marjorie made a little curtsy. Clearly she had choreographed this: curtsying was such a Marjorie thing to do.

The ache in Sarah's heart was so piercing that it might have been caused by a dagger. She actually looked down at herself, not really surprised at being intact, but surprised by the fierceness of her longing, by the way missing someone could hurt so much.

She thought about calling, but decided against it. It seemed cowardly. But as she approached Marjorie and Joey on the far side of the soccer field the next day at lunch, she wondered if twelve-year-old girls ever had heart attacks. If your heart could pound so hard that it left bruises on the inside of your chest. If what felt like fear was really just weeks and weeks of not watching old movies, not laughing at old jokes, not remembering things that had happened in second grade.

Marjorie and Joey were sitting on a bare patch of dirt, their backs against the chainlink fence that marked the most distant edge of the field. Marjorie was holding half of an oversize sandwich in one hand. Sarah imagined that barbecue potato chips made the bread look lumpy.

The two were talking and laughing, but as Sarah came nearer, she could tell that Marjorie was aware of her, that her speech became less animated. Finally she looked up. With her free hand, she pushed her glasses up the bridge of her nose. Sarah tried to read the expression on her face and couldn't. Was she angry, upset? She looked unbothered, but something in the emptiness behind her eyes let Sarah know that she was masquerading, only pretending to appear serene.

Sarah slowed her pace but forced herself to come close. Be brave, she had said to Lizzie at the choir party. She tried to say it to herself. Was it working? She didn't know: her heart still banged uncomfortably against her ribs. But she went on, her sneakers squeaking a little in the damp grass, her fists clenching and unclenching in the front pocket of her hoodie.

"Hi," she said, coming to a stop before them.

"Hi," Marjorie and Joey said together. Joey looked from her to Marjorie, then back at her again, as though he thought Marjorie might lunge at her and try to wrestle her to the ground.

"Can I talk to you alone?" Sarah asked.

"Sure," Marjorie said. She took an enormous bite of her sandwich, then set it on top of the plastic grocery bag that contained, Sarah knew, the rest of her lunch. She rose from the ground. "Tell everyone to wait," she said to Joey through a mouthful of sandwich. "I'll be back in a minute."

Sarah steered them several yards away, toward two metal garbage cans locked to the fence with metal chains looped through their handles. She tried to think of something to say as they walked, but found herself tongue-tied. How many times had she and Marjorie walked and chatted effortlessly? Thinking of something to say had never been a problem. In the old days, the problem had been not enough time to get all the talking done.

They came to a stop in front of the garbage cans, over which two bees buzzed lazily back and forth.

"So who's 'everyone'?" Sarah asked, surprised at herself, feeling jealousy like a vise around her lungs.

"Some kids Joey knows. Davis Lindemood. Peter Hurley." Marjorie wiped potato chip crumbs from her mouth with her bare arm. "We're starting an anime club," she said, smiling a little, as though she couldn't resist telling.

"I miss you," Sarah blurted out. It sounded so full of ache and wanting that she added immediately, "I miss how it used to be."

"I know," Marjorie said. "Me, too."

For a moment Sarah felt hope shimmer around them, fragile and iridescent, a giant, wobbly soap bubble that would keep them safe, would shut out everything.

"Me, too," she said, echoing Marjorie, not wanting to say anything else, wanting to live in the bubble just a moment longer.

"You can be in the club, if you want," Marjorie said.

The way Sarah had known that she would.

"I don't really get anime," she said.

"You could if you tried," Marjorie said. "If you read enough graphic novels. Watched movies."

"What I mean, I guess, is that I don't really *like* anime," Sarah said. "I mean, it's okay. And it's fine that *you* like it—"

"Don't," Marjorie said. "It's okay."

Sarah could hear the faintest tinge of irritation in her voice. For some reason, it made her feel better.

"Why can't we go back to the way it was?" she asked. "When we had lunch together every day and watched old movies and laughed all the time?"

The bees were buzzing too close; reflexively, the girls began to walk again, hugging the edge of the field, taking slow steps, as though by slowing down, they might put off some sort of ending.

"I like eating with Joey and Davis and Peter. I have fun with them. We like the same things. We laugh at the same things," Marjorie said. "The way you like eating with Lizzie and Carly."

"Not Carly anymore."

"Well, Lizzie, then."

"Lizzie's really nice, Marjorie," Sarah said.

"I know. But—"

"But what?"

"Nothing." Marjorie shook her head and pushed at her glasses. "Nothing."

They walked on. Marjorie swatted at something to the side of her head, as though one of the bees were following her.

"We can still be friends," Sarah said. "We can still have sleepovers and watch old movies and talk on the phone."

Like hedging a bet, she thought.

"Yeah," Marjorie said uncertainly after a moment. "We can still do those things."

It sounded awful, much worse than yelling at each other, saying they hated each other, crying, calling each other names. Sarah knew how awful it was because it was a lie to try to pretend that nothing was different, nothing had changed. Sarah knew it, and she knew that Marjorie knew it, too.

Marjorie always knew.

"I don't get why this happened," Sarah whispered. It felt as though it was her fault, as though she hadn't paid enough attention. Another promise broken, she thought.

"Maybe it's just *supposed* to happen. Like getting taller," Marjorie said. "Only no one told us."

Sarah nodded, afraid to agree out loud, too close to crying.

"I have to go back," Marjorie said, half pointing to where Joey sat with Davis and Peter. "They're waiting for me."

"Okay," Sarah said. "I have to find Lizzie, anyway."

They shared a long look. Sarah forced herself not to try to pretend anything. Be brave, she said in her head. The truth of what was happening ached in her heart, in her bones. But she didn't turn away.

Heading back toward the schoolyard, she couldn't resist taking one more look. Marjorie was trudging toward the small knot of boys at the back fence. Sarah could hear their distant, gleeful shouts as she rejoined them.

Making her way through the hallways, she saw Lizzie and Robert and Jason crowded together. For a moment she pretended that she had made a different choice. But when Lizzie glanced up and, catching sight of her, called out, "*There* she is!" as though everyone had been wondering, she knew that she had done what she had to do. She smiled at her friends and felt true pleasure at the sight of them, despite the fierce and terrible hurt still lodging in her chest.

"You almost missed lunch," Lizzie said. "Where were you?"

She mumbled something, not quite answering, and let herself be lulled by the others' conversation, which had something to do with ants. Robert insisted that they were impervious to all insecticides, which led Jason to wonder how many he could swallow at one time.

"You're crazy!" Lizzie cried.

"They're just protein," he said, pretending not to understand her shrieked distress as he knelt down and began to inspect the hallway.

When Mr. Mayberry came out of his room and said wearily, "There will be no eating of insects, Mr. Webb," they all laughed, even Sarah, who knew that they would laugh about it for a long time, that it would become a well-loved memory, like so many others, good and bad: an inextricable part of who she was.